# Nowhere Else To Go, but Dyea

# Nowhere Else To Go, but Dyea

A novel by
Nita Nettleton

Lynn Canal Publishing
Skagway, Alaska

# Nowhere Else To Go, but Dyea

Copyright © 2015 by Nita Nettleton

Cover Art © by Courtenay Birdsall Clifford

All rights reserved. No part of this book may be used or reproduced by any means, graphic, electronic, or mechanical, including photocopying, recording, taping, or by any information storage retrieval system without the written permission of the publisher, except in the case of brief quotations embodied in critical articles and reviews.

Copies may be ordered from:
Lynn Canal Publishing
at
www.skagwaybooks.com
or
Skaguay News Depot & Books direct line: 1-907-983-3354
PO Box 498-LCP, Skagway, AK 99840

ISBN: 978-0-945284-14-7

Distributed outside Skagway by Epicenter Press in the USA and by PR Distributing in the Yukon/Canada

Printed in the United States of America

*To Skagway, for being so deliciously windy.*

*Publisher's Note*

*This is a work of fiction. While Dyea and Skagway and all the other Alaska-Yukon communities named are very real, all other names, characters, places, and incidents herein are either a product of the author's imagination or are used fictitiously, and any resemblance to actual persons living or dead, events, or locales is purely coincidental.*

# 1

The *M.V. Malaspina* arrived late enough to put a hustle in the passengers carrying and towing luggage off the ship. Anyone with very far to go before dark had to get a move on. The basketball team carried sleeping bags and pillows and met parents at the top of the ramp with dragging feet and exaggerated weariness. They had ridden the ferry off and on for over a week, sleeping on gym floors where they played teams from other schools in their league. An old couple was met by a young woman with two small children. The old woman scooped up the suddenly wailing smaller child and carried her to an idling car in the no parking area of the parking lot.

A man with hands jammed in the pockets of a dark winter coat and a black watch cap pulled down over his ears stood aside while his fellow passengers clomped down the steps from the cabin deck to the car deck. He waited until several cars drove up the ramp before he left the ferry, carried a small suitcase across the floating dock, hiked up the covered walkway and into the Skagway ferry terminal. Even after spending most of the three and a half day trip from Bellingham on deck, the cold wind tearing at his face was a surprise. He had a small inside stateroom on the ferry, but could only stand to be in it for actual sleeping. The tight space, metal walls and utilitarian layout was less appealing than the huge, gray and unjudgemental gloom outside the ship.

The man had always been good at remembering important details, so knew to look for someone everyone called His Honor who would probably be in the terminal. There were three people holding signs inside the terminal where passengers made a left toward the parking lot exit. The signs had the names of an inn, a b&b and a hostel. A slightly stooped man with a huge grizzled mustache and wearing a black top hat and judge's robe held the hostel sign and had just directed a young couple to a waiting shuttle outside.

The black watch cap man made an assumption. "Your Honor?"

His Honor's face broke into a thousand lines around a smile. "Yes, sir! How can I help you?"

"I need a ride to Dyea."

"Well, now." His Honor's face sagged. He leaned around the man to glance down the walkway to the ferry. No one else was coming up. "You the last of it, then?"

The man looked around the room. Everyone else was gone or on the way out the door. "Guess so."

"You, ah, want to go right now or after you look around town a bit?" His Honor seemed to be sizing the man up, looking for clues.

The man understood. He was a stranger alone in a small town in the middle of winter with hardly any luggage. Anyone would wonder where he was from, did he understand what going to Dyea meant and, frankly, did he have any money. "No hurry, I suppose." He pulled a slip of paper from his front jeans pocket and handed it to His Honor. "Here's the place."

His Honor took the paper and frowned as he studied the hand-drawn map. "Why, that's the old Winchblatt cabin. Are you sure that's where you want to go? Nobody's lived there much in a good while. It's kinda rough." He handed back the map. "What'd you say your name was?"

"Stillwater." The man reached out his hand automatically. "Henry Stillwater."

His Honor's face was stuck in the frown as he, also automatically, extended his hand. While they shook, he stared, perhaps looking for any reason why this man would want to go to an abandoned cabin at the end of an unkempt driveway in what was left of an abandoned gold rush town at the end of a fjord on the southeast coast of Alaska. In February.

"I think we can get you out there today, Mr. Stillwater. I've got some pressing business here in town, but my associate is headed out there anyway and can take you." His Honor reached under his robe for a cell phone. "He's a firecracker named Darwin." He dialed and held the phone to his ear as he pushed open the door toward the parking lot.

Henry ducked into the men's room, set down his bag, leaned over a toilet and threw up his lunch. After washing his face, he told himself in the mirror that everything was working and he was on track. He went over in his head what he learned from Allan, the crewman on the ferry who grew up and still lives on the road to Dyea. The ferry lands in Skagway, a gold rush boomtown that thrives on tourism, and a highway leads north out of town and into Canada. The Dyea Road snakes west along the shore to the head of the fjord the ferry came up. Dyea was also a boomtown, but didn't survive the building of a railroad out of Skagway. Now it's a quiet river valley with a handful of homes. Nothing to be worried about.

His Honor was fighting to put the phone away under his billowing robe when Henry forced the door open against the north wind. After just a short time indoors, his face was shocked again by the icy blast.

"Darwin's on his way. He's got some firewood for Ms. Walton, your neighbor, so you and she can split the cost of the trip. In cash." His Honor still regarded Henry's face with keen interest with his head tipped into the wind to keep positive pressure on his hat. "You sure you want to go out there?"

Henry thought a moment and said, "I have nowhere else to go." He knew for some time that his options were limited, but had never actually said it before. It felt sad and desperate on the one hand, but fairly solid on the other. Clear direction is clear direction.

"Well, that's the case for many of us, I suppose. You'll be needing some supplies."

"Yes, I'm sure I do. But until I see the place, I won't really know what."

"Hmh. Just a guess, but you'll need everything. Have Darwin run you by the grocery and hardware. He says he knows the house and what you'll need. This your only bag?" He pointed to the lone suitcase Henry had set on the curb where the luggage cart had parked before going back onboard for the layover in port.

"Yes, that's–" Henry paused, then stepped back as he watched a pickup truck roar through the parking lot and loop to a quick stop in front of the two men. It was an older blue Ford with rust around the entire bottom edge of the body. The right front fender, the one that stopped about a foot from Henry's left hip, was a clever amalgam of sheet metal and plywood. A homemade slatted crib in the back held cut and split firewood.

"Good luck, Mr. Stillwater. I hope I'll see you around." His Honor touched the brim of his hat and hurried in a chaotic flapping of black fabric to the only car in the parking lot.

Darwin hopped out of the driver's seat and spit deftly with the wind on his way around the back of the truck. His ball cap didn't budge at any point along the circuit nor when he lifted his stubble-bearded chin sharply by way of greeting. The two men regarded each other for a moment. Darwin stepped around Henry and picked up his bag, swinging it up on top of the firewood in one smooth arc. "Ready?"

Henry didn't feel ready. He didn't like being separated from his suitcase which contained all he had left, even as far as the back of the same vehicle he was going to ride in. He took one slow, deep breath and opened the door. The passenger seat of Darwin's truck was not very inviting. He still thought of himself as a large man and didn't think he'd fit in the narrow space next to a stack of flat cardboard crates. He managed to squeeze in and when he pressed against the crates to close the door they started cheeping. At least a hundred tiny voices filled the crates by the volume and complexity of the cheeping.

The pickup left the parking lot under a dense, low cloud cover and started up a nearly deserted street between Victorian style buildings. Henry knew Skagway was small and he'd arrived in the off-season, but didn't expect it to be this inactive. There was no sign of life on the street. Darwin called over the cheeping, "Hardware store then grocery, okay Mr. Steeplewhite?"

"Henry. Actually, there is one more stop I need to make and should probably do that first."

"Sure, Hank, what's that?"

"The police station. I need to check in." Henry looked at Darwin, but saw no change in the boy's neutral expression.

"Yep. Right around the corner." Darwin slowed and did a U turn in the street, jogged one block right, left, and pulled up in front of a small, modular building with the withered remains of last summer's petunias in pots along the front. "I'll wait."

"Thanks. Should just take a few minutes." Henry gently disengaged from the cheeping crate tower and slipped out. He gasped when the wind hit the side of his face and hurried for the door.

A skeletal, red-haired woman with very pale skin and a Skagway

Police Department uniform looked up at Henry with owl eyes enlarged by her huge glasses. "May I help you?"

"Yes, ma'am. My name is Henry Stillwater. My parole officer said he sent you my information." The woman gave no indication that she understood or would respond. A small wave of nausea sloshed in Henry's stomach as he fished in his inside coat pocket for a set of folded papers. "I have copies." He handed them over the counter and concentrated on his breathing, hoping the Zoloft he took after breakfast was still on duty and didn't eject with his lunch. The woman took a full five seconds to lift a pale hand and take the papers. She scanned down the pages.

"We got your stuff. I started a file. Do you have ID?" Henry got a thin wallet from his jeans hip pocket and gave the woman his Texas driver's license. She looked at it carefully, glancing up to compare the photo to Henry. "You've lost weight. You'll need to come in every three months and fill out a form, any employment information or travel. You'll be in Dyea?"

"Yes. I'm headed there now."

She leaned toward the window. "Hmh, Darwin. Watch that kid." She handed back the license and papers. "You're at the old Weinstien place and the name on the title isn't yours. Who is the owner?"

"My daughter, A. J. Her name is really Yvonne. Yvonne Banks-Stahl."

The woman's face brightened, as if slightly interested. "Your daughter is also your attorney, then. She called this morning. Said to tell you she opened an account for you at the bank and they've sent you a debit card. Too late for the bank today, though. You got some cash?" She peered over her glasses to see Henry nod yes. "You'll be wanting an Alaska driver's license. Come in any time."

"Yes, ma'am." That seemed to be it. Henry nodded and left. He wondered if A. J. made that call herself or had someone in her office do it.

## Nowhere Else To Go, but Dyea

In the cab of the truck, Darwin had taken off his Carhartt jacket and wrapped it around the crates. The cheeping was down to a murmur. "Was that Hilda?" At Henry's blank look, he described her. "Red hair, ugly, old, real snoopy?"

"Yeah, that was her." Henry blew out a breath and relaxed into the seat. The first step was done. On to the next. "The guy in the judge's robe said you'd know what I need, but let's just keep it bare bones." As the truck began moving, he glanced at Darwin. "Is he a judge?"

"Nah. Used to be the magistrate, about a million years ago. Always wears that getup. Now Hilda's wicked stepsister, Ruthless Red, is the magistrate." Darwin rolled his eyes and shook his head.

The hardware store filled an old building on the main street. Darwin parked against the boardwalk directly in front of the door and both men dashed to the recessed entry. Inside, a dog sleeping in front of a pile of sacks of ice melt didn't move when the door banged shut. Darwin knew his way around and quickly set a flashlight, package of lamp mantles and a can of lamp fuel on the counter. He looked over stack cleaner options and chose a pack of the sticks. To Henry he said, "you got a little soot problem."

Henry knew the cabin had no electricity, but hadn't considered what he would cook on. He hoped it wasn't the wood stove. After Darwin told him there was a cook stove he asked if he needed gas for it and suggested things like a can opener, pots and dishes. Darwin shook his head to each item, saying, "Got it."

At the grocery store they wheeled a buggy down all five aisles and filled it about halfway, mostly with cans of food just needing to be heated up. They added toilet paper, matches, paper towels, and trash bags. Darwin asked, "Can you afford all this?"

Henry glanced down at his clothes a little self-consciously, reminded for the thousandth time that he didn't look like he used to. Anyone might wonder if he could afford groceries. He realized that

Darwin would also be concerned about collecting his delivery fee. "How much are you charging me?"

"Thirty bucks."

"And thirty bucks from Ms. Walton for delivering her wood?"

"Oh, right, Ms. Walton. Okay, twenty for you since we're shopping, too."

Henry didn't really know why he asked about Ms. Walton since her commerce was none of his business. Twenty was probably more than fair for all the help he was getting. "Okay, we're good." Darwin nodded and suggested some dairy products.

"Is there a fridge?" Henry didn't expect appliances of any kind.

"It's February. The whole outdoors is your fridge."

Henry paid cash, just over $85, for what he hoped would last about two weeks. He'd been warned to expect high prices. Even so, $85 would have been a cheap lunch date in his old life. The grocery sacks settled around his feet in the pickup cab as they left town on the Klondike Highway. They turned west onto the Dyea Road. After about a mile, Darwin stopped in front of a house close to the right side of the road, put on his coat and eased the wildly cheeping crates out. He said he'd be right back and dashed to the house. A man answered the door and took the crates inside. Darwin followed but was back out in about a minute. He ran back to the truck, stuffing cash into his pocket. The Ford nosed back onto the road. Soon the pavement gave way to gravel and they rattled along in waning daylight. The limited view between the trees of Long Bay and then the Dyea valley at the head of the fjord softened. Bare birch trees and gray green conifers parted now and then to reveal gray water down below. The steep hillsides disappeared into thick gray clouds.

Henry remembered seeing a few still photos of Skagway on the Chamber of Commerce website. What he saw today was nothing like the lively shots of brightly colored buildings, people and cruise ships framed by snow-covered peaks. He couldn't imagine anyone wanting to vacation in the landscape he saw on the Dyea Road.

By the time they turned off the main road and threaded through the forest on a one-lane road, it was nearly dark. Darwin slowed and hugged the right side of the road to squeeze past a small car with no headlights on. He gave a discreet fingers-off-the-top-of-the-steering-wheel wave. It was the only car they'd passed since leaving Skagway.

Henry felt a renewed wave of unease as he glanced over at Darwin casually steering the old truck between huge tree trunks. The boy, about as down home blue collar as it gets without an active plug of tobacco, had a serene calm about him. And he was taking Henry deep into the woods. Henry Ford Stillwater thought he had explored every nuance of helplessness over the last two years, but this was a new one. His immediate situation had the classic childhood red flags: lost in a cold, dark forest, at the mercy of a possible axe murderer. Not that he had actually seen the axe, but he was sure there was one. In the back or under the seat. There was always an axe.

## Nita Nettleton

# 2

Henry's anxiety backed off a few notches when the hulking, dark trees gave way to a wide, twilit yard. He could see a ghosty, sagging tepee to one side, a woodshed to the other and a lumpy but solid looking cabin in the middle. Another structure was partially blocked by the cabin, maybe a greenhouse. Clumps of not-quite-melted snow rimmed what he presumed to be the south side of the clearing. Darwin stopped the truck in front of a set of steps onto a wide porch that ran the width of the cabin.

"I'll help you get settled then take this wood over to Mr. Walton." Darwin pitched his head to the left. "That's her light you can see through the trees. She's your closest neighbor, you lucky bastard." He chuckled and hopped out.

Henry slid out of the truck and stood for a moment looking at his new home. It clearly was not all built at the same time. The original was most likely the log part, about twelve by sixteen feet, then a section about the same size was added, board and batten sided, to the east. The porch looked newer yet and ran the length of the south side. The windows were unbroken and the smoke stack stood straight. Much better overall than expected, Henry thought.

He had heard a description years ago during a lucky poker game at a Rotary convention, then saw the plat when he got title after the card game loser's funeral. The plat only showed the original cabin and a small outbuilding. Henry redrew the plat in his head and was sure the outbuilding was in the same spot as the woodshed. He gathered his grocery sacks out of the truck and followed Darwin who carried the suitcase and fuel can up the steps, down the porch and through the unlocked door. Darwin used a Bic from his pocket to light a candle on a cupboard inside the door.

"There's a little wood in the shed for now, but I'll bring you more if you want me to add you to my route." Darwin took the chimney off an Aladdin lamp sitting on the table in the center of the room. "You know how to put on a mantle and use one of these?" He noted Henry's head shake, then quickly installed one of the new mantles, filled the lamp and lit it while Henry watched. The lamp flared and settled and the room came alive. The kitchen was very basic, but had a sink with a small pitcher pump on the side, gas stove and counter space with shelves above and below. There were pots and pans as well as stacks of odd dishes and cups. Even a stack of folded towels. A very worn orange shag rug covered the main room floor.

"Bedroom's in there," Darwin said, "clean sheets. The outhouse is out back, be sure to take a roll of paper. I'll get you a fire started." Darwin used newspaper and kindling from the box beside the wood stove and a few pieces of split wood stacked behind it to lay a fire. He opened the damper, lit and waited. "Just watch the draft for now, you can use one of those sticks and clean the stack tomorrow when you can keep an eye on it. Not a bad stove."

Henry watched the lively flames through the open stove door until Darwin closed it. "Um, someone's obviously been living here. Recently."

"Well, nobody's really lived here for awhile." Darwin adjusted the stove damper. "Don't close this too far. You need anything else? I should get this wood over to Ms. Walton."

"No, I . . . here's your twenty bucks." Henry handed over the cash and sighed. "Home sweet home."

"Yep. A guy could do a lot worse." Darwin started for the door. "Oh, the pump." He went to the sink. "Keep the handle up to drain the pipe when it's cold. You just prime it." He took a quart mason jar from the back of the counter and poured it in the top of the pump while he worked the handle. After about four strokes, water gushed out. "Don't forget to fill the jar before you let the water column drop. And don't let your prime water freeze. It's been warm lately."

Henry studied the pump and went over the process again in his head. "Is it safe to drink?"

Darwin shrugged. "There's a spring out by the road a lot of people use for drinking water, but others use this."

As Darwin opened the door, Henry called to him, "Thank you for your help. Better put me on your firewood route."

"Will do, Hank."

Darwin turned his truck around and bumped down the driveway, now totally dark under the huge spruce and hemlock trees. Henry carried the Aladdin lamp into the bedroom and a tiny side room that served as storage closet. He opened the back door and could see an obvious trail that led behind the outline of a greenhouse. In the bedroom, he turned back the blankets and sheet and leaned down to sniff the queen size bed. He picked up a pillow and sniffed. Smelled fresh. He wondered how an unlived-in house could be in such good shape down to clean linens. In the kitchen, the pots and dishes were all clean. Henry got the box of matches out of a grocery sack. He lit one and passed it around the burners while he turned each of the knobs on the front of the stove. All burners lit. Amazing, he thought. He expected to be basically camping out. On very limited funds, it would have taken him a long time to fix up the house to this standard. With wonder, gratitude and a growling stomach, he put away his groceries and opened a can of green beans and a can of chili to heat for supper.

After eating and washing the dishes, Henry used his new flashlight to find and use the outhouse. Again, much nicer than he expected. Inside the cabin he looked over a bookshelf in the living room stuffed with a wide variety of books published in about a hundred and ten year time span. The house was warm enough to take off his coat. He hung it on a hook by the door. He thought about the fire in the wood stove, so put the coat back on and went out to the woodshed. He gathered an armload of wood and brought it in. Coming back to the house he noticed there was no wind here like there was in Skagway. Inside he relished the warmth and soft yellow lamplight. Maybe this won't be so bad, he thought. "Step two, done," he whispered. He opened his suitcase on the bed and took out his shaving kit and a notebook. The notebook had a pen in the spine. He sat at the table, put on reading glasses, opened the notebook, slid the lamp a little closer and began an entry in his journal for February 25. He had gotten a lot of counseling over the last two years and whether he wanted to hear it or not, everyone insisted he keep a journal. That it would help. He had to admit now that it did. A common thread in his journal from the start was that he wanted to crawl into a hole and die. He flipped back a few pages and noticed that his writing was slightly less gloomy since starting on Zoloft, getting on the bus, reaching the coast and riding north from Bellingham on the Alaska ferry. He looked around the room and wondered if this was the hole he'd wished for. If so, as Darwin said, a guy could do worse.

Henry slept soundly and long. He did wake once, with a start. He thought he heard the latch on his cell door clunk close, but as his heart rate settled down, he was pretty sure it was a tree branch slapping on the metal roof over the bedroom. The wind had come up. In the morning there was a light rain. After a trip to the outhouse and breakfast, Henry did a thorough walk around the buildings. The woodshed had splitting tools and a snow shovel. Judging by the amount of wood he'd burned overnight and in the morning, there was enough for a couple of weeks. A large propane tank sat on a pallet outside the kitchen wall. Henry had no idea how to judge how full it was. He'd have to ask Darwin. There was a spade and rake in the greenhouse and raised beds with good-looking soil. Whatever grew there last was still there, withered and brown and hanging down over the sides. Clay pots were stacked in a corner with moss beginning to grow in them. The tepee was empty. It had a canvas cover, not hides, Henry was relieved to see. Mostly dry inside, grass and small bare twig shrubs extended a couple feet into the doorway. The house itself showed good and recent care. The caulk between the logs was intact, front and back doors latched and sealed well, all windows were fairly well caulked and there was a rain gutter along the porch roof. A fishing theme thermometer hanging on one of the porch posts read 45 degrees. Someone lived there recently or visited regularly, Henry affirmed for the hundredth time. Darwin's truck tracks from the evening before were hardly noticeable among all the other tire tracks. That can't be good, part of his brain thought. Other parts didn't know.

After the rain, the air was fresh and cool. Henry stood a good while in the middle of the yard listening to and smelling the forest. He heard squirrel chatter, bird cawings and a very deliberate "God dammit!" The last was a woman's voice and came from the direction Darwin had pointed out Ms. Walton's light. He heard a loud thunk, like a heavy object being thrown or whacked against something, then "Varmits!" Henry had believed he wouldn't have any neighbors, but clearly he did and not very far away. His lot, he remembered from the plat, was about two acres. Where he grew up, that was practically a farm. But, now within swearing distance, he had a neighbor.

The storage room in the house had window cleaner, a broom and dust pan. Henry swept the whole house, dragged the rug outside to drape over the rail and whack with the broom, cleaned the counter and table, wiped out the drawers of the little dresser in the bedroom, cleaned the mirror over the dresser and swept the porch and steps. Along the way, he found two hooded sweatshirts, a pair of slippers, sweatpants and one each men's and women's underpants. He hung the clothes on the hooks by the door and set the slippers below. He noticed they looked about his size. The corner of something stuck out behind the bookshelf. He slid out a framed drawing of an old-style electric fan. Something about an image of an electric appliance in a house without electricity felt poignant to him. Finding the nail likely put there to hold it on the wall over the bookcase, he rehung it. He swept out the outhouse. Looking around outside again, he realized he was very lucky the snow had melted. This time of the year, there could easily be a lot more. Back inside, he put away his clothes and arranged his shaving kit contents on top of the dresser. He read the directions on the smoke stack cleaner and followed them with one of the sticks. It burned hot and fast and he wondered if it was such a good idea, but then it settled down. One more thing to learn: how to maintain a wood stove. He'd used wood heaters at ski chalets and hunting cabins, but never as a home heating system. And they'd often been set up for him; all he had to do was strike a match. Or his daughter would strike the match. She was such an ourdoorsy kid. Who would have guessed she'd follow in her mother's footsteps through beauty pageants to become a lawyer. Even as a baby, though, she looked just like her mother. Henry called her A. J. for Anne, Junior.

An engine sound took Henry away from the wood stove and to the window. A white and blue police cruiser came into the yard and stopped. Henry was grateful there were curtains on his windows as he ducked back to peer around one of them. A tall, uniformed, bare-headed man got out and walked to the porch. He had all the normal police gear on his belt, but walked casually, more like a regular person than a police officer. He climbed the steps, walked to the door and knocked.

Henry took deep breaths, willing his nerves to settle. One of his counselors told him this was a common feeling; that even after years of freedom, some people had fear of being rearrested and going back in. He had nothing to worry about, he whispered to himself. He did everything he was supposed to do. His paperwork was in order.

"Mr. Stillwater," the officer called out. "It's Dave, Skagway PD. Nothing to worry about, sir. Just a courtesy call."

Henry could feel his blood slow down. Apparently Dave knew about the anxiety thing. "Just a moment," he called, hoping his voice sounded unworried. He opened the door wide, like a regular person, not afraid of a stranger at the door. "Hello."

"Good morning," Dave smiled and waited on the porch.

Henry reminded himself a regular person would invite a stranger in, maybe offer coffee at this hour. "Won't you come in?" He stepped back and waited for Dave to walk in, then closed the door behind him. "Coffee?"

"Thank you," Dave said. He walked to the table and sat in the chair that didn't have a coffee cup sitting in front of it. "I smelled coffee from outside, must be pretty strong."

"Um, it is. I haven't perked since college." Henry took a cup from a shelf and poured from the percolator on the stove. He was relieved his hands were steady and the pour was smooth. "I don't have anything to put in it, since I drink it black. I guess I should have thought of that."

"Not a problem, I take it black." Dave took a sip after Henry handed him the cup. "Mm, that is substantial." Dave smiled, set the cup down and let his eyes bounce around the room. "The place is livable?"

"Yes," Henry sat at the table. "Much more than I expected. I thought it had been vacated years ago and would be full of raccoons or . . . bats, I guess. But you'd know a lot more about that than I do."

"Mm." Dave slouched down and stretched his long legs out straight, crossing his ankles. "No raccoons around here." He rested his cup on top of his slightly rounded belly. "The original part of the house is quite old. Not gold rush old, but homesteader old. Then it changed hands and someone fixed it up enough to live in again, but they left. The folks who moved in around the early seventies brought the tepee and used the house, too. They left and a couple from Juneau added on, built the greenhouse and sunk a well. But they found out they were on the wrong property. They really owned a place further back in the valley where the sun never reaches. Kind of blew the wind out of their sails. They were only ever here weekends, anyway. Then . . ." Dave sipped coffee and thought. "Then Darwin's dad used it as a hide-out from his wife and kept it up. He drove off the Dyea Road one night. Then no one spent any time here until a couple years ago. Kids from town took an interest and cleaned it up, use it for a time-out place, I guess you'd call it."

Henry tried to follow the parade of owners or squatters, but took particular notice of the last users. "You saying kids have kept clean linens and dishes?"

"These ones will surprise you. Some mischief now and then, but overall good people."

"Do they know I'm here? Will they want their stuff?"

Dave smiled. "Everyone knows everything, you can count on that. The kids know you're here and they may want a few things. I doubt much. Legally, it's yours. Most of it's garage sale dishes and forgotten furniture." He held up his coffee cup. "I remember a set of these at the community rummage sale about three years ago. And your rug came from one of the hotel remodels. Not a recent one." He stretched and stood up. "I should get going." He looked down at Henry. "Will you be all right here?"

"It's a big improvement on my last lodging." Henry stood. "I wanted a quiet place out of the way and this is about as far away as it gets, I imagine."

"Sure feels like it in February. Not so in July, but you've got time to ease into it. Will you be looking for work?"

Henry snorted. "No one is going to hire me to do what I know how to do, Dave."

"Well, a lot of folks here are doing just about the opposite of what they knew how to do. We may have the best educated bartenders and tour guides in the world." Dave took a card from his shirt pocket. "Call me if you need anything."

Henry took the card and nodded.

At the door, Dave turned. "I should tell you the reason I came out this way today. Ms. Walton, your neighbor to the west, called last night to rip me a new one about letting a sex offender move in next door to her." At Henry's horrified look, he hurried on. "I told her you're not and she has absolutely nothing to worry about, but thought you should know. When you meet her, just let her vent until she runs down, then she'll be reasonable. Makes one hell of a rhubarb pie."

"How did she even . . ." Henry was still shaken.

"Aw, that little shit Darwin told her you checked in at the station before you came out, she drew her own conclusion. Not his fault, really. She'll weasel information out of you and then fill in what she doesn't get, so you may as well tell her. Up to you. If you can stand her, you two could probably help each other out. She really shouldn't be driving anymore and you'll want a ride to town now and then. And, as I said, very righteous rhubarb pie. Anyway, feel free to call me."

Dave left Henry with a new worry. He closed the door and sat at the table. Sex offender. Great. He read Dave's card and asked aloud, "How would I call?" Then he remembered Dave said Ms. Walton called last night. So she has a phone. And she has electricity since that was a bright light at her place and he didn't hear a generator. Not only did he have a neighbor he didn't expect but there were utilities in the area. Contact with the outside world could be easier than he thought. Or wanted. He wondered why A. J. didn't say anything about that. Maybe she didn't know. She could have chosen not to tell him. She was hard to read even as a kid. And they hadn't been close in twenty years. Longer really; since she was about twelve. He'd been busy creating a financial empire while she was busy creating her own world. He put her through law school and she never even thanked him. But when he suddenly needed very good legal help, she was there. Maybe she agreed–no, insisted–that he let her represent him out of a feeling of debt. Early in the process he wondered if she planned to screw him, too, but as the trial began he saw how hard she worked for him. He believed he would have spent a lot more time in prison and in a less appealing one with anyone but her leading the team. He knew it. And there wasn't much else he knew anymore.

In his journal, Henry briefly described meeting Dave and how little it took to make any feelings of security and control erode into dread and worry. He hated feeling so volatile and was embarrassed by it. He had always been a man with a plan, and whether or not the plan worked, he always had confident direction. He flipped to the back of his journal and looked at two pages, each with a heading and nothing more. A therapist suggested he make a list of goals and a list of steps toward the goals. He sort of had the steps started and wanted to have something to check off. He made a column of numbers, one to ten, and began writing steps from the top. The first step was *get to Skagway and check in with the PD*. Check. Next step was *get to Dyea and settle in*. Check. Nothing occurred to him for a third step. He suspected he was getting his cart before his horse and looked at the goal page. What were his goals? Well, one he knew was important to do before he died was to make peace with A. J. Their relationship in prepping for and getting through the trial was strictly professional. He didn't see her afterward but worked with her staff. He wrote that down as goal number one. Number two, according to his head rather than his heart, would be to forgive Claire. She had signed on as the proper accessory to a prosperous man. It wasn't her fault. He didn't believe he could ever forgive Anne and his former business partner whom she now lived with, but maybe someday he could forgive himself. He still wasn't sure if he was more angry or embarrassed about losing everything and going to prison. And was it about breaking the law or about getting caught? The same therapist who suggested the lists also asked him if he would do it all again in the same circumstance. No. Yes. Maybe. Back to goals; surely he had more. What does a person do to move on? How do you begin rebuilding? He wrote, *make at least one new friend*. Then, *find something meaningful to do. That doesn't involve finances*, he added. He looked over the entries and thought they may not be in the best order. Maybe the first one should be making a friend. He would have to think about that.

Thin, white sunlight reached into Henry's house. He looked around the room and liked what he saw. It was nothing like anywhere he'd lived before, but that was nice in a simple way. He loved the quiet. The sofa in front of the south window had a sunbeam slowly grazing across it. The upholstery was worn, but the colors were richer in the light. He realized he had not sat on it yet. He got up and walked back and forth in front of it, then sat in the center. He sank down and leaned back. It was very comfortable except for a lump under his tailbone. He reached back to feel what the lump was and pulled a small hard cover book from behind the seat cushion. The cover was dark green and the title and author were embossed in it. It was Robert Service's *Rhymes of a Rolling Stone*. Henry put on his reading glasses, opened the book and began reading.

# 3

By Saturday morning, Henry was getting the hang of things. He felt comfortable with the water pump and the wood stove. He'd bathed and shaved and hand-washed some underwear and hung it to dry. He had walked to the edges of his property and was pretty sure he found the corners. He'd gone through all the books and picked out several he planned to read. He was becoming a fan of Robert Service. Many of the characters in Service's poems were outcasts, men worn raw by circumstances of their own making but outside their control. And most of them survived. A soft thump on the porch Friday morning drew him to the window to see a massive cream-colored dog get comfortable and take a nap. It happened again Saturday morning. Henry kept an eye on it, but didn't get involved.

Darwin came by with a load of firewood and helped Henry stack it in the woodshed. He said Henry could pay him when he got into town and to the bank. He could run a tab. Before Henry could stop the words coming out of his mouth, he asked if that was such a good business move.

"Well," Darwin told him, "the guy I used to deliver for just got a job with the Park Service. He turned over his customer list to me with his saws and splitter. All I have to do is keep his woodshed full for a year. Now I cut all the wood myself, but no cash out of my pocket and I control the whole business. You need wood and aren't going anywhere so you're a sitting duck for my competitor who might try to sell to you. You wouldn't care who you buy from. As I see it, it's in my interest to keep your woodshed full. How's your propane holding out?"

Henry couldn't fault the kid's logic. It was pretty good business. "Propane? I don't know. How do I tell?" They walked to the back of the cabin and Henry learned to look for the frost line on the outside of the tank when it's cold or to rock the tank and judge by the weight. It was a twenty-gallon or one hundred-pound tank and Darwin judged it to be about half full. He said it should last a couple months, anyway, unless he did a lot of baking or was too lazy to keep the wood stove going and lit the burners to heat the house.

Darwin hefted the crescent wrench welded to a chain looped through a heavy eye bolt screwed into one of the cabin logs. "My dad had a thing about having a wrench when you need it." He smiled. "He set this up. You turn off the tank when it's empty, disconnect the line and take it to town to get it filled. You meet Ms. Walton yet?"

Henry looked up from mental practice with the wrench and tank valve. "No."

"Too chicken?" Darwin struggled to hold a serious face.

"Yeah, kind of. Dave, the cop, was here the other day and said you told her I had to check in with the police so she assumed I'm a sex offender."

Darwin snorted a gust of laughter. "No shit!"

"No! You made her sound scary enough, but now I'm terrified of her."

With considerable effort, Darwin straightened his face. "Ah, she's not so bad. You just say 'uh huh, uh huh' and let her run on. She always argues both sides of everything with herself, so you don't have to say anything. You could get a ride to town with her, easy. Only you should drive, man, she's dangerous. I don't even like to come out here Wednesdays and Sundays when she's on the road."

"She just gets better and better," Henry said. "Not saying I am, but if I were to go meet her, do you think I should go asking for something or offering something?"

"Asking. She'd be suspicious if you're offering."

"I guess I could ask her about utilities. What she pays for phone and electricity."

"That'd work. Except she's been fighting with both companies for years and you'd get an earful. You want phone and electric?"

"Maybe. I don't know. Why not?"

"Well... it's not cheap, but really it's just so peaceful here without it."

"It is that."

Darwin took a cell phone out of his jacket pocket. "You could get a cell. It works up at the pullout usually. Or way out on the flats. And in town, of course, and the rest of the known universe." He put it away. "You be able to pay me next week?"

"I'll make it a priority."

Darwin nodded. "Work it into your busy schedule. Everything else okay?"

"Oh, two small mysteries." Henry pointed to the cabin. "I found a few pieces of clothing someone may want back, and there was a huge dog on the porch for about an hour yesterday and again today."

"Yellow, crooked tail, one flop ear?"

"Yeah, maybe."

"Her name is something sissy, so Esme calls her Serious. Because she's so serious, I guess. I'll ask around about the clothes."

Darwin got in his truck. "Oh, Belva at the post office said to tell you to come get your packages."

Henry waved as the truck drove off and wondered what could possibly be waiting for him at the post office. Then he remembered it was his birthday. Not that anyone would send him a present. It was the first birthday he'd ever spent all alone. After his parents and friends hosted annual parties for him, it was his wife and friends, then his wife, daughter and friends. A. J. always liked that he was born on Leap Day, February 29. She thought he would live forever with a real birthday only every four years. Usually they celebrated it March 1. Later he shared birthdays with his staff and friends or with Claire, then, the last two birthdays, his cellmates. Henry tried to think of one person who might be missing him today and he couldn't. Those bridges all burned. With the money.

"Well, I do need to get to the bank. May as well get it over with," he said out loud. "Just go over, knock on the door and say, 'Ms. Walton, I'm your new sex offender neighbor and it's my birthday. I'm 'dog dirty and loaded for bear.' " It was the only line he could quote from Robert Service, but it was a good one. He went inside and cleaned up.

The way to Ms. Walton's was down the single lane driveway between tall spruce trees and sharply to the right, up another single lane driveway. The yard at the end of the drive was a smaller clearing than Henry's but the house was larger. It was two-story with dormer windows upstairs, wood shingles on the roof and a narrow porch across the front with a fancy rail. As Henry got closer he could see the blue paint was faded and beginning to peel. A matching garage sat to the right of the house. As he approached the porch, the garage door began to rise with a whirring sound. He could see taillights then the rest of the back of a Honda Civic. The car lurched back in an arc to the left, headed for the spot Henry stood on. He took several quick steps and hopped onto the first porch step. The car stopped suddenly and the driver's window lowered. The face looking out at him was like no other Henry had seen. A snorkel mask sat above a wide, open mouth with red lipstick. A multi-color knit hat covered the rest of the head.

"Hello!" The wide mouth widened further into a smile. "You must be Hal, my new neighbor! I was just coming to see you and bring you a pie. Hold onto your hat, I'll try to get back into the garage." Ms. Walton hit the gas and rammed the Civic back inside the garage, braked suddenly and rocked to a stop. She turned off the engine, got out and carefully slid sideways between the side of the car and floor to ceiling stacks of boxes. Her arms were over her head holding something wrapped in a flower print towel. She came to the porch and looked up at Henry. He could see she was wearing glasses under the mask.

"Huh. You're taller than Darwin said." She leaned a little closer and dropped her voice. "You should know he's telling everyone you're a sex criminal." She worked her way up onto the porch, reaching with each foot to find the steps. "Warm out today, isn't it? I called Dave to report Darwin, he shouldn't be saying things like that, and Dave said you like music." She stopped and faced him. "I said, who doesn't like music?" She threw her head back and let out a long, very musical laugh. "Come on in!" Henry followed her through the door and into another world. The front room had a wood floor covered with a large oriental rug. The furniture, including a piano, was old, ornate and stacked with magazines, books and teacups in matching saucers. A stairway on one side of the room went up, each step holding a stack of books. French doors in the back of the room were open to a kitchen with a huge, black old style range with chrome trim. Ms. Walton bumped into a wing chair and stopped. She set down the towel-covered bundle and carefully lifted her mask up and off. Her hat went with it, releasing a wild mop of sunny curls. She set the mask and hat in the chair and turned around to face Henry. At rest, her face had webs of fine lines around her eyes and mouth. The leading edge of hair at her temples was white. He considered speaking while she studied him, but decided not to.

"So, not all that tall." She shrugged out of her coat and draped it over the chair, then picked up the towel bundle. "Come into the kitchen, I'll make tea. You can try this pie." As cluttered as the front room was, the kitchen was neat and tidy without stacked books. Henry was invited to sit at a small table. He took off his coat and hung it over the back of the chair before sitting. Ms. Walton hummed something that sounded familiar to Henry while she put a kettle on the stove and got out plates and cups.

"The kids are doing the 'Pirates of Penzance' this year and, thank God, I was asked to help, but it's a real challenge. None of them sings very well. Still, they're learning their parts and it should be a lot of fun to watch. The costumes are wonderful. Jean makes all the costumes and they're always beautiful." She set two small, ornate forks and matching spoons on the table with cloth napkins and a sugar bowl that matched the plates and cups. She poured the tea and plated two pieces of pie. "So, how are you doing over at the Warrenchuck place?" Henry had the first bite of pie on his fork and halfway to his mouth. He paused to answer the question, but needn't have bothered. "Well, I was good friends with Mrs. Warrenchuck, bless her heart. It was such a shame what happened to them. The good part was that they had applied for electricity, but the lazy bastards hadn't gotten to them yet when they moved out. They would have needed only one pole and that would have been a lot cheaper than I had to pay with my two. Then there was the prorated whatever and all the excise blah, blah for crying out loud." She stopped and closed her eyes while she chewed a bite of the pie. "Mmm, this rhubarb pie is from the freezer and I forgot it has beets, carrots, apple and nuts in it. You're not allergic to nuts, are you,

Hal? The beets really boot the color." Ms. Walton sighed and looked at Henry. "You can use my laundry if you want to. It's right through there," she pointed to a door off the side of the kitchen, "help yourself any time. Just don't put any of that commercial detergent crap in it or I'll have to run a cycle to clean it out. Use the stuff I have. Better for you. Dave said you don't have a car, so you'll need a ride to town. I go on Wednesday and Sunday. Be ready on time. You can't use my bathtub, it's upstairs. You don't have a bath over there, do you? I hope you keep a pot of water on the wood stove so at least you have hot water for washing." Henry didn't have a pot of water on his wood stove. That was a good idea. He was heating water as needed to mix with the cold for shaving and washing. He opened his mouth to say so, but was cut off. "I've got just the pot for you in the garage. You can get it out. I think it's on the top shelf on the right side, toward the back. There's a short ladder out there if you need it. Darwin said you were tall." They drank their tea and finished their pie in comfortable quiet.

Henry set down his fork. "Thank you, Ms. Walton, I don't think I've ever had pie this delicious. And was that licorice tea? It went very well with it."

Ms. Walton purred. "You're too kind, Hal." She stood up. "I'll wrap the rest of this for you to take home. Now when you get that pot down from the shelf I need you to look for a dead squirrel in that corner and get it out of there. I hit it with a rock. They steal insulation, you just can't let them move in. Then they have a family and you have more of them taking your insulation and God knows what all." Ms. Walton got up and wrapped the pie. Henry put on his coat and followed her back to the door and outside. She navigated much more surely down the steps without the snorkel mask. She set the pie on the step and waited outside the garage while Henry threaded his way up the right side of the car, stepping over and around gardening tools, boxes and several fist-sized rocks. In the back corner there was a step ladder and he could see a large black enamelware pot on the top shelf. He positioned the ladder and started up, but stopped with a jolt when he came face to face with the dead squirrel clinging to the outside of a box. On closer inspection, the squirrel was the back end and tail of a fox fur hanging from the rim of the box. He tugged and the front end came out, head and all. It was the kind of fur women used to drape around their shoulders, usually two or three skins clipped together. Henry squinted and tried to imagine what the half fox looked like from the garage door through a prescription snorkel mask. He tucked the whole thing inside the box.

He shifted his weight to reach the black enamel pot. Trying not to dislodge more dust than necessary, he slid it out and lifted it down to chest height. He was pleased to see it had a lid. He had just begun to step down when he heard a whoosh and something clunked him on the head and fell down to the floor.

Ms. Walton called from outside, "Are you okay, Hal? Is that the squirrel?"

Henry held the pot in one hand and reached up with the other to carefully touch his head at the impact site. He didn't feel any blood. "Everything's okay, I just dropped something." He stepped down to the floor and looked at what hit him. It was some kind of a wood box. He set the pot on the hood of the Civic and leaned down to pick up the box. He turned it over as he picked it up and was surprised to see a smiling baby lying in a mat of straw. It was a Nativity scene piece. "I knocked down your Christmas decoration, Ms. Walton. I'll put it back up."

"My what? Let me see." Henry worked his way along the car stepping over the rocks and holding the manger over his head. He turned it so Ms. Walton could see. She stared, open mouthed. "That's . . .that's . . . Oh my God!" She dropped to her knees and made the sign of the cross. "It's the missing Baby Jesus! Oh my

God! They'll think I took it! Oh my God! We need to work fast. Here," she stood up and opened the back of the Civic, "put it in here. We'll cover it. And we'll take to the church tomorrow. Yes, that's what we'll do. Oh my God, I can't believe it. It's been missing for years and here it is in my garage!" She jerked her head to the right and peered into the trees. "Someone put it there." She closed her eyes and took a few deep breaths. "Well, what's done is done. Did you find the squirrel?"

"Uh, yes, ma'am, I did. I'll get it. You want me to just toss it in the woods?"

"Yes, that's fine." Henry went back into the garage and Ms. Walton walked toward the porch, talking to herself and gesturing with her hands. He got the enamel pot and squeezed back out. When he got outside, Ms. Walton was facing toward him, so he swung his right hand in an underhand pitch toward the woods, launching the imaginary squirrel. "Good, that's done," she said and held up the wrapped pie. "Bring back the dish after you've washed it. Be here at ten tomorrow for church. You can drive."

Henry walked slowly down the drive and back to his house. As goofy as his first contact with Ms. Walton was, it was positive overall. And he had a ride to town tomorrow, although the bank wouldn't be open on Sunday. Nor the post office. Maybe while Ms. Walton was at church he could walk around and get a look at the town.

## Nita Nettleton

# 4

After checking the wood stove, Henry ate another piece of Ms. Walton's rhubarb pie. He'd never been much of a fan of rhubarb, but this was surprisingly good. He ate it slowly, thoroughly tasting each bite. On the ferry coming north, he'd seen good-looking pie in the case in the cafeteria, but didn't buy any. He was concerned about having enough money to get to Dyea and into a livable situation. It had been so long since he'd had to worry about how much cash he had in his pocket, just the having to worry made him worry. It had been an uncomfortable trip because of it. He looked around the warm cabin and acknowledged he felt much better now. Next week, next month and the rest of his life were not sketched out very well, but now was secure. Maybe that was all that had ever really been secure. The couch and Robert Service called to him.

*Henry dreamed that he and Anne were Christmas shopping. She couldn't decide whether A. J. would like diamond or emerald studs for her first earrings. He had lost interest and wandered to the perfume counter. A pretty young woman named Claire helped him choose a scent for his daughter. He bought the one he liked the best on Claire.*

He could still smell it when he was startled awake and listened.

There was a light rapping on the door. Henry got up off the couch and went to the window. A small, dirty car sat in the yard and he could barely see the curvy backside of someone standing close to the door. He took a breath and opened it.

"Hi. I'm Esme." Esme held out a small, pale hand poking out the end of a loose, pink sleeve. "Welcome to Skagway. I mean Dyea, I guess."

Henry took the small hand and gently shook it. "Thank you." Esme looked about twelve years old to Henry, but her short, unnaturally red hair, modest makeup, nail polish and well developed shape made her obviously older. She wore tiny emerald stud earrings. She wrapped her arms around her ribs and shivered. Henry reacted like a father. "It's cold. Won't you come in?"

"Thank you." Esme walked into the room and looked around as Henry closed the door behind her. Her eyes went wide when she got to the clothes hanging on a hook by the door, next to Henry's jacket. "Oh my God!" She hurried over and reached up, grabbed the clothes and quickly wrapped them into a bundle, underwear to the inside. "Where were these?"

Henry almost reported truthfully that he found them under the bed, but thought better of it. "I don't know, in a drawer, I guess. I can heat up some coffee if you'd like a cup."

"Um, sure." Esme kept the clothes clutched to her ribs and perched on the edge of a chair. "Nice here, isn't it?"

"Yes, it really is." Henry lit a low fire under the percolator. "Do I have you to thank for it being so livable?" She just shrugged her shoulders, so he added, "If there's anything you want to take, please . . ."

"No." She smiled a little and relaxed further into the chair. "Everything here belongs here. Except this stuff." She indicated the bundle in her lap with a shy laugh. "Darwin called me when he picked you up the other day, so I ran out to clean up. I passed you guys on the way in. No, we just brought stuff here as we needed it or when there was no place else to put it."

"Who's we?"

"Oh, me and Darwin, mostly. Sometimes other kids. We come out – came out – to do homework and . . . whatever." She laughed. "My mom thinks I do homework with the TV and music on, but I really can't. Well, easy stuff like English I can, but not my stupid geometry." She turned to the bookshelf. "In fact, I think I left my stupid geometry book here." She got up, clothes still clutched to her middle, went to the shelf and looked. "You straightened this all up. Here it is." She took a medium-sized textbook out and carried it back to the table. Henry poured two cups of coffee.

"I should have told you I don't have any milk or sugar."

"You've got something better," Esme said as she went to the kitchen and reached with her free arm to a shelf crowded with mugs. She pulled a small box from behind the mugs and set it on the counter. "I hid it. I'm pretty well addicted to this mixed into coffee. I hope it's strong coffee." Her face suddenly looked several years younger to Henry.

"Swiss Miss with mini marshmallows? Yes, ma'am, coming right up." He got a spoon, opened a pouch and stirred it into one of the mugs. He carried both to the table. "I've got rhubarb pie, too, if you'd like some."

She laughed and sat down. "No, thanks. I had about all the rhubarb I could stand a long time ago. It's kind of a weed around here." She closed her eyes and sipped her mocha. "I needed this." She sighed and opened her eyes. "So you've met Ms. Walton."

It was Henry's turn to laugh. "Yes, this morning. I was not looking forward to it, from what I'd heard, but I came away unscathed." He remembered the whack on the head with the Baby Jesus and reached up to touch the spot. "I got a lump, but no blood."

"She threw a rock at you?"

"No, she nearly ran me over with her little car, but missed. Then she gave me pie and tea, offered me her laundry facilities and gave me that big pot to keep water on the wood stove. She asked me to remove a squirrel she killed with a rock in the garage and something fell on my head."

"She killed a squirrel with a rock?"

"No. But I didn't tell her. Is rock throwing her claim to fame?"

"Yeah, I guess. Everyone's got a Ms. Walton rock story. She's such a goofball. But really . . . her claim to fame would be her beautiful voice. Have you heard her singing yet? Sometimes you can hear it from here while she plays and practices. I guess it's more in the summer with the windows open. She sings like an angel." Esme had a euphoric look on her face. She took a drink of her mocha and her eyes caught on the geometry book. Her cherubic face turned to stone.

Henry saw the change in her. "What's so stupid about geometry?"

Esme slumped. "Everything. I just can't see it, you know? I try to memorize enough to get a decent grade, but it's driving me insane. Darwin can see it, but I can't. And he can barely read." Esme looked up apologetically. "I don't mean that, he can read, it's just miserably hard for him. He's kind of dyslexic. Do you know what that is?" Henry nodded. "So I try to help him with his English and he helps me with math. But, even though he can see the angles and the shapes in his head, he can't explain them to me . . ."

Henry remembered when A. J. was in high school and fighting her way through geometry. She was a whiz at speech and theater and led the debate team, but couldn't see the logic of geometry. She never asked him to help her with her homework and only heard about her difficulty later when she needed a summer school class to graduate. His brilliant A. J. needed summer school. He tuned back in to Esme's story.

"... so I need a good grade to get the scholarship. It just sucks."
Henry reached for the book. "Mind if I take a look?"
"Go ahead."

There was a stack of papers folded inside the front cover. Henry opened them flat on the table in front of him. Worksheets and quizzes were marked up with red pencil. "Where are you now in the book?"

"Well," Esme flipped through the textbook. "The class is up here, and I'm back here." She was about three chapters behind. "I have until Easter break to catch up." She drummed her fingers on the book. Her black polished fingernails were chewed to the quick. "My dad died in the fall and the teachers are letting me work at my own pace, take more time where I need it." She flipped a few pages. "I always did real well in school and it would just kill Dad to see me failing like this. So ... Wait, you're some kind of hot finance guy, right? You could help me."

Henry couldn't believe what he heard. "Excuse me?"

"I work at the police station two days a week after school, it's a cadet thing for extra credit. I heard Hilda and Dave talking about you, that you were some big corporate money something. You probably do this geometry stuff in your sleep."

"Esme, I . . . went to prison over corporate money something."

"But, not because of geometry."

"No, not geometry." He turned the papers over, scanning down each one. "I guess I could look through this and . . . Leave your book with me a day or two and I'll try to come up with a better way to approach it. It's not really math, it's all about logic. Got me through my teens, actually." He looked up and saw hope in Esme's face. "I'm really sorry about your father."

"That's okay, he'd been dying for quite awhile. It was good to get it over, really. It's just that life is so different now for Mom. Not so much me." She stood up and re-gathered the bundle of clothes.

"Can I come back on Wednesday? Monday and Tuesday are my PD days."

"I may go to town with Ms. Walton on Wednesday."

"Oh, right. She goes in early now to work with the drama group, then shops and gets to choir practice at the church at six. Maybe you could meet me at the library while she's at the church?"

"Okay. That will give me time to work something up."

Esme jumped up. "I feel better already. I'll see you Wednesday!" She flew out the door and was gone.

Henry felt drained. He ate another piece of pie and lit the lamp to start in on Esme's geometry book. As soon as he sat down he felt restless. Why did he agree to help her with her homework? He didn't even know her. Plus, something nagged at the back of his mind. It was something the sentencing judge said about staying away from anything to do with money, in a nutshell. Well, math homework isn't necessarily about money. And, as he said to Esme, geometry really isn't about math. He got up and paced a few laps around the room. He needed to get out and breathe fresh air. It would be dark soon, so he slipped the flashlight in his coat pocket, put on his boots, hat and gloves and headed down the driveway. As he passed Ms. Walton's drive he heard music. He stopped to listen. It was a very lively piece, maybe from the kids' play. He didn't hear any singing, just the piano. He walked on out to the larger public road and turned left. He figured if he only made left turns, he couldn't get lost.

It was fully dark when Henry got to a bridge over a churning, swishing creek. He could see ice along the edges, but free flowing water otherwise. The air temperature felt a few degrees colder on the bridge. He turned back, made the right onto his road, but instead of the next right into the drive he shared with Ms. Walton, he kept going. There was no moon, but he could see the basic shapes of the landscape. It felt good to walk. The road twisted back and forth and the trees thinned. He passed a silent campground on his left and crossed a small bridge. He went on, following the worn tread of the road to a wide, open flat area. He guessed he was at the head of the fjord. Dark mountains to either side and behind, absolutely nothing out front. Stars appeared one by one overhead. Tentatively at first, then with a little more muscle in it, a band of pale green lurched and wobbled across the sky. Henry was transfixed. He'd seen the northern lights once on a Boy Scout camping trip in Maine. They'd been green like this. As Henry watched, the green band suddenly grew and morphed into a ring. Rays shot upward to a focal point and the whole thing pulsed and shimmered like a huge, slo-mo fireworks explosion.

## Nita Nettleton

# 5

    In the dream, Claire was trying to decide what to wear to a benefit dinner. She tried on several dresses and asked Henry to pick the one he liked. He said more than once, "Wear the one you like, Babe." He finished dressing, put on cufflinks, tied his tie, and she was still standing in a pile of discarded outfits. Obviously, she waited for something from him, but he didn't know what. So he asked, "What?" She stomped into the bathroom and slammed the door.

    Henry got up in the thin light of dawn to finish work on Esme's geometry before going to Ms. Walton's. He stirred up and fed the wood stove and started coffee. As he made the bed, he noticed how feminine the pink sheets and coordinating spread and bed skirt were. Who uses bed skirts anymore, he wondered. Then he had an unsettling thought about what the mattress may have been through with all the people who'd used the cabin over the years. He quickly pulled off the linens and was relieved to find a fairly new-looking and clean mattress cover. He lifted a corner and peeled it back. The mattress was a popular brand and in good shape. In the middle there were several dark speck- to dime-size spots. Henry lived with women long enough to recognize female blood stains. The rest of the surface was unmarked. He felt relief. He picked up the edge of the mattress and hefted it high enough to get a look at the underside. It was clean. He remembered his first night settling into what would be home for at least eighteen months and possibly twenty-four in the Eloy, Arizona federal prison. In temporary lock-ups, he'd learned to get a good look at the mattress. The lockup mattresses had a colorfully wide range of body fluid stains. Both sides of his Eloy mattress had spots he didn't want identified in several shades of yellow.

For a moment, Henry debated whether or not to flip his current mattress over. Anyone would want to sleep on a totally unstained bed, but suddenly that seemed a little sterile. Even lonely. He thought of a practical reason not to flip it; save it for when you need it, he told himself. He quickly redressed the bed, making sure the skirt hung evenly.

Lamp light grew and warmed the room around the table holding Esme's book, papers and his steaming coffee cup. Henry looked at the worn rug and couch, the odd lot of books, the log walls and the homemade door. He hadn't thought about it before, but the door didn't even have a lock. This house, clearly, had a much more interesting life than he had. There would have been periods of quiet. Maybe sadness. He wondered if a house ever felt lonely. Sitting in the warm and quiet house, Henry didn't feel lonely.

He read through the geometry chapters to get to where Esme was stuck. Geometry hadn't changed much in the last few decades. Not having any other paper, he used blank pages torn from his journal to make notes and drawings. A scuffling on the porch got him up to look outside. It was the big yellow dog, turning in circles, sniffing, then trying a new spot on the porch, circling and sniffing. Henry opened the door. The big dog walked in, went to the middle of the rug, turned in a circle three times and flopped down. The thermometer on the porch read 38 degrees and felt chillier than the day before. The dog appeared to be sound asleep and didn't move at all when Henry came back in, closed the door, whispered, "Seriously," and went back to work.

A list was forming in Henry's head of things he needed, but it did not include long underwear. He picked up two sets while out shopping with Jason, one of A. J.'s law clerks. The young man had never been outside of Texas and Florida, but knew you needed long underwear to live in Alaska. They got most of what Henry needed for his new life at a huge sporting goods store near the airport in Dallas. Jason was sure a gun of some kind was necessary, too, but had no idea how a convicted felon could travel with one. There was a big store-wide sale associated with a boat show and they had to work around a crowd of people buying everything from fishing rods to camo print bikinis. Henry got expedition weight underwear tops and bottoms, socks, mid-weight hiking boots, a warm coat, hat, gloves and two flannel shirts. He already had jeans, shorts, tees and a robe. He couldn't imagine that he would ever need dress clothes again. Everything he wasn't wearing fit easily into a modest suitcase. He had never traveled with so little, let alone set up housekeeping. The last trip he and Claire took was a short week on Malta. For that he had one huge duffel and a small wheelie. She had twice that.

Henry went over the list on the walk to Ms. Walton's. He was glad he had brought warm clothes, since that had been a big enough expense in Texas. Surely clothing costs a lot more in Alaska. What he needed now was stuff like pencils and paper. He could use more toothpaste. Listening to Serious snore on the rug all morning, it occurred to him a battery powered radio for news and music would be nice. The big dog followed him out the door when he left the house, but went her own way somewhere beyond the woodshed. Maybe he should get a box of dog biscuits.

Ms. Walton was ready to go when Henry arrived a few minutes before ten. She greeted him with a quick, musical good morning as she stuck her arm out the door to hand him the key to the Civic. Her hair was up in a bun and her lipstick perfectly matched a deep pink sweater. She closed the door in his face. He used the garage door opener dangling from the key fob, squeezed alongside the car and further squeezed his large frame into the driver's seat. Once in he could see there was a man door into the garage from the house, but it looked like it would only open part way between towers of boxes. No one bigger than Ms. Walton could use it. He started the car and carefully backed out. Ms. Walton, in a sky blue knitted hat, hopped in the passenger side and settled a wicker brief case and her snorkel mask on her lap. Henry closed the garage door and asked her if she minded if he moved the seat back. She smiled, assured him she didn't at all and thanked him for asking. He reached for the release and began sliding the seat back, but it wouldn't go far. He reached further under the seat and closed his fingers around something fuzzy. It wouldn't budge. He scooted just a bit forward and it dislodged. He pulled out a brown and cream spotted cowhide purse.

"Oh! I've been looking all over for that!" Ms. Walton took the purse and set it on top of her briefcase. Henry scooted his seat as far back as it would go.

The sky was brighter than it had been since Henry arrived and he could see the tops of the near mountains and far down the fjord. The shoulders of the mountains were rounded and forested, but the peaks were sharp and covered with snow. The road to Skagway was all twists and turns along the convoluted shore, so he never drove faster than about twenty-five miles an hour. There were a few driveways leading up into the forest on the hillside or down to the beach and a few houses were visible. Henry had to keep his eyes on the road, but couldn't help noticing the scenery and wonder about the people who lived in it. Ms. Walton chattered nonstop and covered several local topics: Dyea Road improvements, about a dozen tragic car wrecks, including Darwin's father's, avalanches on the Klondike Highway, weekly barge service into Skagway, and the cost of groceries. She got a little worked up over the last item, but took a few breaths and calmed down. When they stopped to turn right onto the Klondike Highway, she began in a conspiratorial tone to go over how they should deliver the long lost Baby Jesus to the church.

"I've given this a lot of thought. I was going to have you wait until after the service starts and no one is looking to slip it into the rec hall, but that would not be the end of it since everyone would wonder, then ask around, then whoever put it in my garage would know that you took a cowardly way out in returning it. Then I thought we could drop it off at the Catholic church since no one is there this early on Sunday unless the priest is in town. But I couldn't remember if he's here this week. So I decided the best thing to do is to ask Kevin to come out to the car, we tell him everything, ask where he wants you to put it. And ask him not to mention me. Then he can thank God during the service, do one of those clever double meaning things he likes to do about the missing years and Christ being risen to segue into the plans for the Easter program. I worked out a choral arrangement for the Mozart piece I've been practicing, everyone's going to love it. Don't you just love how we get several minutes more daylight every day this time of year? There's no fellowship after church today. Just as well since I don't have what I'd need for deviled eggs until Wednesday. So we can go home at noon."

Henry followed directions to park the car on the curb in front of the rec hall on 5th Street, next door to the church. He got out and waited for Ms. Walton to go find Kevin. A biting cold wind made him take his watch cap from his pocket, put it on and pull it down over his ears. A few minutes later, she came out with a young man in slacks, shirt and tie with sandy hair and beard. Kevin offered his name and hand and began to ask Henry about himself, but was interrupted by the opening of the Civic's back hatch and the careful peeling aside of a wool blanket.

Kevin stared and sucked in breath. "Oh, the Baby Jesus! He's been gone since before I got here. Look, He just glows, doesn't he? So much more lifelike than the replacement one. Let's get him inside, it's cold out here." Kevin gathered the manger into his arms and carried it into the building. Ms. Walton went with him, opening and closing the door. Henry closed the Honda's hatch and waited on the curb. Several cars parked behind the Honda and across the street, people got out and went into the church. More people walked from all directions, some smiling and nodding to Henry, others staring openly, still others pointedly not making eye contact, all entering the church. An airplane landed a couple blocks away. Henry walked around the car to move and try to warm up. There were small dents on all four corners. He still had the key and debated locking the car. On the one hand, most likely no one locked cars here. On the other hand, Ms. Walton was paranoid and might go nuts if he left hers unlocked. Dave had said that everyone knows everything. Henry took a chance and held up his hand to a grizzled middle aged man coming down the sidewalk.

"Excuse me," he held up the car key. "Do you know if she locks her car?"

"Nah," the man shook his head. "Just be sure you're here when she comes out. And bless you for driving, man."

"Right, thanks." Henry nodded and waved as the man hurried on. The stabbing wind was relentless and he looked at the clean, white Victorian church. It probably had a big old furnace cranking out righteous heat. He checked his watch, jammed his hands in his pockets and began walking.

The town of Skagway lies in a very neat grid. Numbered streets cross the narrow valley with 1st at the waterfront. Five named streets run lengthwise. The names are not very imaginative, but, as

## Nowhere Else To Go, but Dyea

Henry knew from refereeing board meetings of several civic organizations, people don't often fight over names like Alaska, Main, State, Broadway and Spring. He wondered at Congress Way, the curved road to the dock, and made a mental note for a museum stop some day when it was open. He didn't find many open businesses. He didn't want to spend any money, but wouldn't mind stepping into a store to warm up. The grocery, a pizza pub, liquor store, hardware and for a very short posted time, the newspaper and bookstore were open on Sunday. He again consulted his watch and decided to keep walking until the bookstore opened. He found the bank next door to the post office. An air service van came out of the alley next to the post office. Henry looked alongside the building and saw a woman stacking packages on a hand truck and wheeling them inside a service door. He wondered if it was Belva. She looked like she could use some help.

"Excuse me, can I help you with this?" Henry stopped by the door just as Belva came out for another load.

She parked the hand truck and arched her back to stretch it then looked Henry up and down "It's the US mail, I can't really let ... Who are you?"

"I'm Henry Stillwater. Just moved here."

"Oh yeah. Stillwater. When are you coming to get your packages? You've got a few pieces of mail, too."

"Well, I don't have a car. I got a ride in from Dyea with my neighbor. So, Wednesday, I guess."

"Tch. I'd like to get it out of here. Give me a minute and you can have it now." She glanced both ways on the alley before letting Henry help her load up the cart and take the remaining packages inside the back room of the post office. She disappeared but came back quickly with several flat pieces in one hand and arms filled with four boxes. "You'll be wanting a mailbox. There are some available."

"I really don't expect to be getting any mail to speak of. Is it okay to use general delivery for now?" He took the parcels from her.

"If you want. Or, and don't tell anyone I said this, you can share with someone else in Dyea and help each other with pickup. It just goes faster that way."

"Okay. Thank you." Henry was glad the wind was to his back as he headed south on the wood plank sidewalk of Broadway. It was clearly the tourist part of town. Several buildings had small plaques with the National Park Service logo telling their original purpose and date they were built. Several of the restored historic buildings had displays in the window, but were obviously closed for the winter. Some had paper over the windows and two had scaffolding against the walls and repairs in progress. Henry felt a pang of sympathy for anyone working on a scaffold in this wind. He got to a spot across from the bookstore just as the open sign flipped. He stopped to look for traffic before crossing the street and recognized Darwin's truck coming. The truck swerved to the edge of the boardwalk and stopped. Darwin hopped out and jogged around to face Henry.

"Hank, what size boots do you wear?"

"Uh, a twelve, usually."

"Good. Hey, did you just get all that from Belva?"

"Yeah, I saw her carrying a bunch of packages in and I offered–"

"Shit, she never gives anyone their stuff on Sunday. Anyway, it's gonna snow and I need a few more loads of wood down before it does. Couple days should do it. It'll be worth your while. You want me to take those boxes? I hope one of them isn't the cake with the file in it, finally caught up with you." Darwin laughed.

"Just my luck. Ms. Walton's car is down at the church."

"You don't want her to see you got mail on Sunday, trust me, we'd never hear the end of it."

Henry leaned over the side of the truck and let the boxes spill into it. "Hope it's not the Steuben glass, either," he said to himself. As a kid he read his mother's copies of *The New Yorker Magazine*, dreaming of a day he would have enough money to live and dress like the people in the ads. The first year he and Anne were married he ordered a Steuben glass etched heart to give her for Valentine's Day. It arrived in pieces and, for several years, was a joke they shared whenever either dropped a box or got a battered package in the mail. He hadn't thought about that in a very long time. He straightened up and tucked the flat mail into his pocket.

Darwin started around the truck to get in. "Pick you up around nine in the morning." He acknowledged Henry's nod and was gone. Henry wasn't sure, but he may have just agreed to help Darwin cut trees and wrestle firewood out of the forest. He had no idea what that was like. He crossed the street and went inside the bookstore.

"Hello!" A woman's voice came from somewhere in the cramped space of bookshelves and a sales counter piled with books and newspapers. "Back here."

Henry pulled off his hat and gloves and followed the voice behind the pile of newspapers. He saw the top of a head of curly gray hair at about chest level. He leaned around the stack to see a fine-boned face with olive green eyes locked onto him over red framed half glasses. She looked academic to Henry and very East Coast. Something about her looked familiar.

"Go ahead and look around," she said. "I need to get these papers organized before everyone gets here to claim them. The Sunday *Juneau Empire* is actually here same day and word of that will get around fast. Holler if you need anything." She went back to work and Henry browsed. There was a large selection of Alaska-themed books and he pulled out and leafed through several Klondike Gold Rush accounts. He'd seen some of the pictures before. The line of people with heavy packs trudging over the snowy pass was a classic. The shop door opened.

"Minerva, I heard a plane. Did the Juneau paper come?" About six versions of the same entry and question played out with Minerva patiently repeating "Yes, here you go" within a span of fifteen minutes. The next person asked for *USA Today* and after that, a man came in and didn't say anything. Minerva simply said, "Yep, here's your *Wall Street Journal*."

Henry put away the book he was looking at. "Excuse me, you carry *The Wall Street Journal*?"

"Carry would be a strong word," Minerva said without looking up. She had a stack of papers fanned out enough to write a name on the margin of each. She straightened up the stack and lifted it down behind the counter. "I just get enough for the people who order it. Not so many this time of year." She leaned her elbows on the counter and, eyes narrowed, looked up at Henry. "Haven't seen you in here before."

"First time."

"Mm, hmm. Yes. You got a ride to Dyea with Darwin on Tuesday."

Henry raised his eyebrows and tilted his head.

"I saw you go by. Actually, what caught my eye was Darwin nearly running over the boardwalk and taking out my sign to make a U-turn in the street. Then you went past again a bit later. The buzz about you runs from thank-God-he's-not-really-a-sex-offender to that you're a Bernie Madoff on the lam. On the plus side, Hilda at the police department thinks you're good-looking and Belva at the post office says you have really good taste. Now, one might wonder if she opens all the packages and can see what you ordered, but I don't believe that. I think she just has a lively imagination." Minerva smiled wide, showing a gold tooth midway upper left. "Someday I'll tell you what they all said about me when I got here. It'll die down and you'll get used to it."

She held out her hand. "I'm Minerva Black."

Henry took her hand gently. She had long, fragile looking fingers with several rings. He was surprised by the strength of her grip as her hardware pressed into his skin. "Henry Stillwater, late of Texas, as you likely already know, now of Dyea," he said. "Uptown Dyea, I believe. I just started reading about it in that book." He pointed to a book displayed and stacked prominently in the middle of the room called *Skagway, City of the New Century*. He'd taken his cabin's copy to the outhouse and left it there for occasional quick reads but didn't mention that.

"Ah! I tell everyone, if you read only one book about Skagway, that's the one."

Henry remembered Ms. Walton and quickly looked at his watch. "I need to go." He reached into his pocket and pulled out a five. "Do you have an un-promised newspaper for sale?"

"I have a *Journal* for you. Someone who orders every issue is out of town." She handed over a fresh *Wall Street Journal*. Henry handed her the five, but she shook her head. "Paid for. He says to give it to the first person asking. That's you. In fact, it's possible I could have another one for you to pick up on Wednesday."

Henry smiled. Of course she knew he'd be coming in Wednesday with Ms. Walton. "That would be very kind of you. I owe you."

"Yes, you do," she said as he hurried out the door. He leaned into the wind and ran the few blocks to the church, arriving just as the doors opened and people spilled out. He got to the car and started it to warm up about two minutes before Ms. Walton came out. She stood and chatted for a minute with a small knot of people, waved good-bye and walked to the car.

"Well, that was lovely," she said, her cheeks flushed from the wind. "I saved a seat for you, Hal. You sure don't need to be shy with this group. Everyone wanted to meet you. Oh, you should have heard the whopper of a lie Kevin told about Baby Jesus coming back." She sighed. "But . . . what's done is done. Do you mind if we don't stop for lunch? Sunday is always split pea or corn chowder and they both give me gas. I'm so excited to get home and work on this music!" She patted her wicker briefcase. "I think we have enough of a choir committed to showing up for practice to actually pull off 'Exsultate Jubilate.' Kevin is a wonderful tenor, but we really need a baritone. Do you sing, Hal?"

Henry checked his speed on State Street and turned to tell Ms. Walton that he hadn't sung since college, but a horrified look on her face made him quickly turn his eyes back to the road and take his foot off the gas.

"That's Squint and little Albedo! Stop, stop the car!"

Henry quickly pulled over and backed up to where a figure was hunched over on a bicycle, toiling up the sidewalk. There was a milk crate on the back of the bicycle and a pointed furry face poked out of a blanket stuffed into the crate. The bike didn't stop, so Henry shifted to go forward and kept pace.

Ms. Walton rolled down her window. "Squint! Are you freezing? Let me give you a ride."

A ski mask inside a hood turned to face Ms. Walton and a cloud puffed out the mouth hole. "Good day to you, dear neighbor. No, thank you, no." The voice was deep and gravelly. "We're out for our constitutional and expect to be home well before dark, yep. How was today's service? I understand the Baby Jesus is returned after a long, inexplicable absence, Hallelujah!"

"Yes, imagine that. I'll see you Tuesday?" Squint nodded, Ms. Walton closed her window. Henry pulled away and sped up. He didn't ask and she didn't volunteer any information about Squint. All the way home, Ms. Walton chatted about the music and the precious few practice sessions before Easter. Henry had tossed his newspaper on the seat before he got in and it could feel its outline. He couldn't wait to settle down to read every word of it. Then he would do the puzzle. With the Civic snug in the garage, he thanked Ms. Walton for the trip, confirmed she wanted to go again Wednesday at precisely noon and walked home.

## Nita Nettleton

# 6

After stirring up the wood stove and lighting a burner to heat up what was left of his morning coffee, Henry flattened and opened his copy of *The Wall Street Journal*. This was a part of his old life that he really missed. The feel of the paper and the smell of the ink went so well with a cup of coffee. The nation, the world and the stock markets all reported in. He rarely got a paper in prison and got used to not knowing exactly what was going on with the Dow and the S&P, but now here it all was. He scanned the price of gold on different world markets along with silver, copper, lead, and zinc. Henry found himself saying hello to the columnists and noticing what was new with the advertisers he remembered. There was no Steuben glass ad, but he noted he wouldn't be able to afford any of the watches, vacations or services he did see ads for. The smell of his coffee boiling caught his attention. He hurried to shut if off and pour a cup before immersing in which governors were in the running for GOP presidential candidates, new findings on the possible extent of Fukishima fallout, the impact of only five thousand black rhinos left on the planet and complications from the Sony computer hack and revelations on trade with China. There were several articles Henry wanted to read again later. He folded the section with the puzzle to be ready to solve.

A quick run to the outhouse reminded Henry that the temperature was dropping. When he got back inside he looked out to the porch and saw that it was just under 30 degrees. He brought in the eggs and cheese he'd stored outdoors, but didn't know where to put them inside. He brushed against his coat by the door and felt the bundle of mail in the pocket. He'd forgotten all about it with the excitement of the newspaper. After a quick decision to put the perishables under the bed where it was cool, he got his mail, carried it to the table and flipped through it. Two letters from Wells Fargo Bank, a letter from A. J.'s office, one from the court in Texas, and one from the Social Security Administration. He opened the one from A. J. first. It was a form letter stating that his account was paid and that he would not be hearing further from the law firm unless he needed help with other matters in the future. At the bottom of the page, Jason scribbled that he had ordered a few more things and they'd arrive by mail. He wished Henry good luck, then added that he should call if there was any trouble with his social security deposits. The bank welcomed him and thanked him for choosing them in the first letter, which included a debit card. The second letter gave him his PIN. The Texas court reminded him that he needed to keep in touch with his parole officer as directed. Social Security advised him he would receive his direct deposits on the third Wednesday of the month. All the pieces of mail were addressed simply to Henry Stillwater, Skagway, Alaska 99840. A small area in Henry's brain noted that there were no birthday cards in his mail, but a larger part was surprised that he was scheduled to start receiving social security. He knew that was coming, but now it was here. Sixty-two years old.

He couldn't stop the follow-up thought that he had nothing to show for it. Not anymore.

## Nowhere Else To Go, but Dyea

He remembered he'd forgotten to take his Zoloft in the morning and got up to get one.

Reheating and drinking the last of the coffee, Henry sat for about an hour digesting what came in the mail and what he read in the news, trying to reconcile it with the room, the cabin, the valley, the quiet chill of early March, and the state of Alaska. He wished he'd gotten a local newspaper, too.

A walk before dinner took Henry out his driveway, to the left to the main road, then to the right to cross the Taiya River. He'd seen a trailhead at the end of the bridge and wanted to see what it was. The sign said Chilkoot Trail. He'd heard about that on Boy Scout camping trips and was thrilled to see it. He walked in, just to see what it was like, followed upriver and up hill past a hikers' register kiosk and up further through huge conifers. It felt good to work his lungs and legs and to thoroughly warm up. He kept going down the other side of the hill, still going upriver past small side channels of the river, bare deciduous trees and shrubs along a very inviting path. He came to a sign at a fork in the trail giving him the distance back to the trailhead: 1.6 miles. A glint of something metallic caught his eye in the matted leaves at the base of the sign. He prodded it with his toe and uncovered a pocketknife. He picked it up and wiped it off. Slipping the knife in his pocket, he turned around and went home listening to birds with unfamiliar songs.

Henry went to bed early after working the meaty *Wall Street Journal* puzzle in ink. He didn't have a pencil. He hoped Darwin wasn't expecting too much out of him in the morning. He hadn't done anything with firewood since he was a kid. His father bought a cord of oak for the fireplace about every other year and it was Henry's job to stack it up the wall in the back of the garage. He read a few Robert Service poems before his eyes drooped enough to promise sleep.

*It was snowing, hard. Henry's dad had staked him the price of a good snow shovel and he went to work after school. He cleared five sidewalks before he recovered the cost of the shovel. Then he was in the black, making money hand over fist. With each walk he shoveled, he fine-tuned his plan for spending it. He wanted a leather jacket, then skis, then a Corvette. When he woke up, he and Claire had just driven into Aspen in the Corvette.*

Darwin arrived a little before nine and drank coffee while Henry tried on the insulated coveralls and steel-toed Xtratufs he brought. When pressed, he divulged they were Esme's father's things. They had both noticed that Henry was about the same size as her dad was before he got sick and shrank. Esme's mom packed everything away and couldn't deal with it yet. So Esme was slowly giving things away to people who could use them. She and Darwin agreed Henry was a perfect match for the outdoor and cold weather gear. That included a fleece-lined flap hat and two pair of work gloves. Henry took a box of granola bars from a shelf to stash a few in his pocket.

"That's not a very manly lunch, Hank. I brought a sandwich for you." Darwin put on his jacket.

"Okay, thanks. I'm taking these anyway." Henry filled a pocket with assorted flavors of oat bars. He'd forgotten about the pocketknife and pulled it out to show Darwin. "I found this on the Chilkoot Trail."

Darwin took it and pried it open. "Hikers drop stuff all the time. This one's nice, just needs work. There's some WD40 in the truck." He handed it back to Henry who was then filling a water bottle he'd found in the storeroom.

"There's a blowdown no one else has claimed yet pretty far up. It'll be a pisser to get to when there's a lot of snow. Which there will be soon."

"How do you know that?"

Darwin just shrugged. "You ready?"

## Nowhere Else To Go, but Dyea

They drove over the small bridge Darwin called West Creek, took a hard left and began climbing up through the forest. There were patches of short growth between the taller trees, like the area had been logged at some point. The narrow, steep road kept them to a slow speed. After climbing for what seemed to Henry several miles, they stopped at a relatively flat and wide spot. The cloud cover was solid and lower here than it had been in the bottom of the valley. Henry inhaled deeply when he got out. The air felt damp and cold. Darwin took a chainsaw and gas can out of the truck. He shoved a file and a few small tools into his pockets.

"See those broken trees?" He pointed up the hillside to a tangle of trees at angles to each other. "Big wind last year. Some are hung up and will be hard to get down, but there's a lot of wood there. We can fill the truck several times from right here." He handed Henry the can of gas and picked up the saw. They climbed up through a jumble of trees, pulled-up root wads and shrubs. Darwin stopped and studied what the wind had left for a full five minutes before deciding where to start. "It's kind of like Pick Up Sticks, you have to figure how to take it apart. I'll cut, you pile it at the truck, we'll load it later."

By noon Henry wanted to die. He had tossed, carried, pushed and cajoled a huge pile of stove length chunks of wood to the truck. Plus, all the branches from the cut trees had to be heaved out of the way to keep a clear pathway. He drank all the water he brought and filled his bottle twice from the little stream below where they parked. He didn't care if he got a horrible disease. His arms were numb and he stumbled back up the hill again and again. Darwin had stopped cutting to fuel the saw and to fix the chain a couple of times, working slowly uphill through the angled trees. At about one o'clock he shut the saw off and set it down. Smoke rose from the hot engine.

"I'm starvin', Hank. Let's eat." Henry watched Darwin hop

from root wad to rock down the hill. He limped after, carrying three pieces of wood. Darwin whistled when got to the truck. "Damn! That's more than two full loads! I didn't know we'd gotten that much. Way to go, partner. I hope you like turkey." Darwin dropped the tailgate of the truck on his way around to get a bag from the front seat. He sat on the gate and took two bundles out of the bag, tossing one to Henry. "You look like shit."

Henry didn't think he could hoist himself as high as the tailgate. He upended a large diameter piece of firewood and sat down. "I feel like shit. You do this every day?" He pulled off his gloves and unwrapped a huge sandwich.

"Not every day. If that asshole I took the business over from had let me know sooner that he was leaving, I would have cut all through fall and been able to take it easy now. But... I would have invested a lot more effort and it's been warm, not so many orders. I would have been left holding a lot of inventory. Not that this shit spoils. We're just lucky there's no snow and we can get up here."

Henry took a bite into a softball-sized blob of turkey, cheese and mustard on a whole wheat bun. It was truly delicious. "Mm, good. So you planned to do all this by yourself now?"

"No, I planned to do it with two of my buddies. But one just got his heart broken, joined the Guard and left town, and the other thinks he's getting a job with the state real soon and doesn't want to work this hard. The wuss."

"Well, I'll be lucky to live through the day." Henry felt like he couldn't get the calories in fast enough. "Reminds me of delivering furniture back when it was still heavy. Big old sofas, sideboards, stuff like that."

"When was that?"

"Summers in high school and into college. Then I learned to tend bar. It was a lot easier and more money."

"How'd you get from there to prison?"

Henry swallowed. "I ask myself that, often." His sandwich was gone and he already missed it. He opened a granola bar from his pocket and ate it. He noticed Darwin watching him, so he offered one to him. He took it.

"You're not gonna tell me?"

"Why I went to prison? Well, basically, I mishandled other people's money and got caught."

"You weren't smart enough to hide some away, like, for now?"

Henry laughed. "No, no I wasn't. I was so un-smart that I even threw all mine in after what I mishandled to try to save it." Henry brushed crumbs from his coveralls. "That brings me to my current situation in a deceased person's clothing, which I'm grateful for, and ready to keel over myself. But maybe not now that I've had such a fine luncheon." Henry stood with effort and pulled his water bottle out of a pocket. "I already drank about a quart from that creek and look forward to more. How quickly is that going to put me out of my misery?"

"Not very soon. I've been drinking it my whole life." Darwin hopped off the tailgate, slid down the bank, squatted and filled his cupped hands several times to drink from the ice-free middle of the little stream. He shook his hands and started up the bank. Suddenly, he clutched his throat and made gagging noises, staggering the rest of the way to the truck. He laughed, grabbed the lunch sack and chucked it inside the cab. He checked his watch. "If you think you can hold off that heart attack a couple more hours, let's cut until about three, then start hauling. And tell me what you think about this. We'll fill up your shed, which is five times bigger than you'll ever need, and use it sort of like a warehouse. I can supply my Dyea customers from there, you have all the wood you need for free."

Henry listened, then said, "No money changes hands?" He had been thinking that he would have receipts for things like firewood to balance not having a mortgage for a tax deduction. Darwin shook his head and waited. Henry extended his line of consideration to the assumption that his income was surely way below poverty level and that a deduction for heating fuel would mean just about squat. Maybe this was a good deal.

Darwin frowned. "Okay, since I'll have to plow snow to get to the warehouse, you get your drive and yard plowed for free, too."

Henry smiled. He hadn't thought about the cost of snow removal. His time wasn't worth much anymore, but a few days of hard labor seemed a reasonable price to pay for the wood and snowplowing. And the less money he handled the better. "Perfect."

Other than wishing for the twentieth time that he had some Aleve, Henry didn't feel too bad after bringing down nearly as much wood in the afternoon as he did in the morning. He was impressed that Darwin noticed there would be an advantage to moving the truck around to a position slightly downhill from the wood pile for loading. He was smart. At least for this kind of stuff. Henry wondered how well he'd thought out his whole business.

On the way down the hill with the first load, Henry began working on his new pocketknife with a rag and the WD40 from the glove box. "If you don't mind my asking, how do you figure your pricing for delivered wood?"

"For now, I'm sticking with the going rate. Wouldn't be right to make changes mid-winter. The supply is never real secure, though, so I may have to charge more next year. And if I need any new equipment. I think that splitter may be shot. But I got a real good Western snowplow set up for really cheap. I'll try to bundle the firewood with snow plowing and other stuff."

"Other stuff like what?"

"Whatever. I shovel snow off roofs, cut nuisance trees, do the dangerous stuff people don't want to do themselves. Small repair jobs."

"Aren't you still in school?"

"Not really. My school career hasn't been what you'd call mainstream. I missed a few years early on, but various people kept talking me into keeping at it. Well, I finally have enough credits to finish, but I have a couple things hanging over my head they say can screw up my graduating. Pisses me off."

"What things?" Henry watched Darwin turn and look at him like he was going to chew him out for being nosy. But they both knew Darwin had already pried to get his prison story.

"A writing assignment and a speech. I haven't started on either one. And I wouldn't even care, but... Esme's all over me about it."

Henry remembered that Esme said Darwin had to work at reading because of dyslexia. "What are you supposed to write and speak about?"

"Well, they're sort of related. I'm supposed to write about the most valuable character trait a person can have and to speak about either home, country or God. I could bullshit my way through any of that with people who don't know me, like the tourists, but everyone at school and the Eagles and Elks knows me. They want the real thing. The clubs are working together on a national speech contest, so that's why there's God in it. The school is almost but not quite making us all participate, but suggesting we talk about home or country. It's my final English grade at stake." Darwin turned into Henry's driveway. "You got any suggestions?"

"Maybe." Henry thought about the Robert Service poems he'd been reading. They were packed with friendship, loyalty and determination as well as home, country and God. Or the tragic loss thereof. "Can you memorize a Robert Service poem?" At Darwin's scathing look he went on. "Strict, proper-form poetry is like a schematic. The right words really only fit in their correct spot. And since it's poetry, people expect you to say it slowly and that gives you time to sort it out. Not a whole, long poem, but just to start out and get you going. And establish a slow delivery. Used to work for me."

Darwin was quiet as they threw the wood out of the truck in front of the woodshed. He planned to bring the splitter tomorrow and they'd stack it in the shed after that. On the way back up the hill for the second load he said, "You could be right about the poem. Everyone here is nuts for Robert Service. My dad was a big fan. I've got his book someplace."

"It's on my sofa. Remind me when we get back and you can take it."

Henry had to work to get out of his boots and coveralls after Darwin left and into a double dose of Aleve. He made a cup of tea and finished the rhubarb pie. He added a mental note to his mental shopping list for food with more protein than he was getting. In prison the food was fairly balanced, but he never ate the pasta and rice because it was always so overcooked. He ate all the meat and vegetables after scraping off the gluey gravy. He took advantage of the facility's exercise equipment to relieve boredom and anxiety more than for any goal of better fitness. At first he couldn't see himself ever getting out of jail and having any kind of a life ever again, so physical fitness was meaningless, but he couldn't sit still and the only outlet was exercising. After awhile it felt good. He lost about seventy-five pounds and four pants sizes. He realized the work he'd done in one day with Darwin was more physical effort than he'd done in decades and would have killed him but for the conditioning he'd done in prison. So, there was a benefit. "'Kid,'" he asked himself aloud, "'Have you been rehabilitated?'" He dipped a pan of warm water out of the big pot on the wood stove and washed up at the sink, humming the tune to "Alice's Restaurant."

Darwin positioned the splitter near the woodshed shortly after eight in the morning, rapped on the door and went in the cabin. He was pouring himself a cup of coffee when Henry came in the back door from the outhouse. "Hey, you lived through the night."

"I guess a downside of living alone is not having anyone to tell you when you're not dead. Actually, I don't feel too bad. Slept like a brick. What's the plan for today?"

"Go get the rest of the cut stuff, start splitting. See how far we get. I have to go in time to meet the ferry. A guy's sending me a trailer full of wood from Haines."

"You're importing?"

"It's a trial thing. He lives out Lutak Road, past the ferry terminal. He's got a lot of wood. So he fills the trailer, puts it on the ferry, I take it off and send back the trailer. I traded a snowmachine for the trailer and the first few loads, then we'll go to cash, I guess. Unless there's something else he wants from here. And we'll have to see how the market goes. There aren't all that many people who buy wood and there's one other supplier. But the trailer is hot because it has clear title. I can sell it easily when I want to." He smiled at Henry, wincing as he climbed into his coveralls. "You gotta watch the details."

With just a quick break for chili and crackers at the cabin, Darwin and Henry had hauled all the wood and split and stacked nearly half before time to go meet the ferry. Darwin left the splitter and said he'd finish it up later in the week. Henry flopped down on the sofa and closed his eyes. Reviewing his shopping list, he thought about what he needed to do to be ready for going to town tomorrow with Ms. Walton. He would go to the bank. The letter from the bank with his PIN said he needed to call a toll free number to activate his card. He hoped he could do that at the bank. May as well stop at the post office again, see if anything else had come. He remembered his packages in a stack by the door. He'd forgotten all about them and sure hoped there was nothing perishable. He got up with a groan and carried them to the table to open. Three were from L.L. Bean and held wool-blend socks, waterproof fleece lined mittens, matching green fleece pants and jacket with some kind of a ripstop fabric over knees, elbows and seat, and a plain black daypack. The box from The Vermont Country Store held a hand crank AM/FM radio. Henry said aloud, "Way to go, Jason!"

Henry's last trip to the outhouse before bed included a swing past the woodshed for an armload of wood. As he gathered pieces, he heard music coming from Ms. Walton's direction. It was piano with singing. He stopped and listened, barely breathing. The voice was a strong, clear soprano soaring and diving, laughing and scolding and taking Henry to a huge, warm cathedral studded with cherubim and seraphim somewhere in Austria.

# 7

After morning chores, Henry found a spot in the cabin where his new wind-up radio got a clear signal and listened to a morning news program from National Public Radio. The station identified itself as KHNS, broadcasting from Haines and serving Skagway and Klukwan. Henry made an addition to his shopping list of an Alaska map. He needed a lot better geographic knowledge of his new home state. Klukwan wasn't on the route map in his ferry schedule, but must be nearby.

He began putting things in his new backpack that he would need for his town trip with Ms. Walton. His new luxury mitts and extra warm hat went in first, then Esme's geometry book with her papers. Flashlight, since he wouldn't get home until after eight o'clock. There was noticeably more daylight than there had been just a week before and he learned on the radio to expect sunset around 6:40. He'd also learned Daylight Savings would start in a few days and boot twilight an hour later. He considered taking his plastic grocery bags back to reuse, but thought he'd need them for trash or lunch bags. Free bags are free bags. One bag already hung on a nail in the closet, slowly filling with washed, flattened cans. Around mid-morning, the now familiar thump on the porch told him Serious was there. When he let her in, she went straight to the middle of the rug for her nap. He'd wondered where she lived, but now wondered if it was a place where she never got any sleep. He hoped the radio didn't bother her. It didn't seem to.

According to the porch thermometer, it was holding at about 28 degrees. The decision to wear long underwear under his jeans felt like the right one as Henry set off for Ms. Walton's a few minutes to noon. He waved good-bye to Serious and she headed off behind the woodshed, apparently refreshed from her nap. The heavy overcast gave the forest a gloomy feel along the driveway. Maybe Darwin was right and it was going to snow. The weather forecast on the radio was for a thirty percent chance of precipitation, but that didn't seem like much.

Ms. Walton again met Henry at the door and thrust out a hand with her car key in it. He opened the garage, put his backpack in the back of the car next to a tidy stack of canvas grocery bags and backed the car out. The driver's seat was still slid back as he'd left it on Sunday. He had forgotten to put it back where she would want it and reminded himself to be sure to do that when they got home this evening. In details, as Darwin suggested and Henry knew full well, lay the way of all things. Ms. Walton came out and hopped in the passenger seat, wearing several shades of green and a light pink lipstick. She carried her wicker briefcase and cowhide purse, but not her snorkel mask. Henry hoped that meant she had confidence in him to get her to town and back.

"Hal, it's such a pleasure to have a neighbor again and one who is on time! That girl last summer, tch." She sighed. "So many people who don't have jobs to go to lose all track of time. I don't guess that matters so much really unless you're late for something. Or early. Which is worse, late or early? I guess it depends on what it is. Oh, look down the inlet, it's so dark! Must be rain or snow coming." They hadn't gotten out from under the cover of big trees yet and she was looking off to the right, into a particularly dense part of the forest. Henry guessed her distance vision was poor to zip. They turned onto the main road and into the open. She brightened up. "Oh, maybe not!" She settled into a contented quiet, humming bits of a tune over and over.

"Ma'am, would it be all right if I came over tomorrow to do a load of laundry?" Henry had a few things he wanted to talk about, but wanted to get the most important item taken care of first while she was in a peaceful mood.

"Surely, Hal, any time, but not before eight. Come in the kitchen door by the garage, it's all there. If I'm working, I won't even notice you, so just let yourself in." She went back to humming.

"Thank you very much." He was going to tell her he heard her singing and playing and that it was spellbinding. But something made him stop. Her manner and body language since he'd met her was baffling. He had no confidence that he was reading her correctly. She seemed tough in some ways, incredibly fragile in others. Even a simple and heartfelt compliment might not go over well. Until he knows her better, he decided, he should stick to business. "Where would you like to go today?"

"The school first for some individual work and a rehearsal, then grocery shopping and soup with my friend, then practice at the church from six to eight. So that's 15th and Main to 4th, over to State, then Broadway below 3rd, back to 5th, over to Main. That's eleven blocks plus two, two back and two more." She smiled, then frowned. "No, no, wait." She closed her eyes and held a fuzzy green mitten to her forehead.

"I'll drop you off at the school and pick you up if you know when I should be back there."

"No, I won't know how long it's going to go. I can get a ride from the school to the store with one of the students, and from there I can walk to the cafe and church."

"Okay. Shall I just park the car at the store? I can pick you up at the church at eight."

"Oh, yes... yes, yes, that will work. You're a breath of fresh air, Hal." She went back to humming.

"I need to go to the bank and post office, would you like me to pick up your mail?"

Ms. Walton glanced and Henry and looked a little agitated. "Well, what would you put it in so it couldn't blow away?"

"I have a backpack. It's behind the seats." He could tell she was listening carefully. "Maybe I could borrow one of your grocery bags to put the mail in, wrap it up and put it in my pack."

Mm, yes. That would work." She reached into her coat pocket and pulled out a key with a bright pink ribbon tied through the hole. "Here is the key. It's box number thirty-two. Be sure it's locked again when you close it." She handed over the key and Henry was careful to put it into his coat pocket. "Don't look at the names, just bring it all. And keep it in your pack, don't leave it in the car." She whispered, "Too risky."

"Got it." Henry had thought about asking her if he could use her mailbox since they were neighbors, but didn't bring it up. "Would you mind if I put gas in the car? It's down to a quarter."

She glanced at the gauges. "Which gas station?"

He had no idea and there must be at least two outlets if there was a choice. "The safer one."

"Good idea." Ms. Walton offered no further advice about gas stations nor money to buy gas with. She directed Henry down Main Street to the school. It was a beautiful, modern building with style elements to complement the gold rush history. A sign identified the school property as Panther Territory. Henry wouldn't have considered a panther for an Alaskan school mascot, but dismissed it as another piece of what he didn't know yet about the place. Ms. Walton hurried for the door without looking back. He turned left on 10th to get to Broadway, turned right and parked in front of the bank.

Inside the warm, old-fashioned looking bank, Henry got as far as introducing himself and presenting the letter describing his account with his new card to a smiling teller. He asked if he could use the bank's phone to activate the card and further asked if he could get a balance on his account. The lone teller's smile disappeared. She asked for identification and he showed her his driver's license. She said she needed two pieces of ID. Henry was relieved he'd decided to carry his passport rather than leave it in an unlocked house in the middle of nowhere. She frowned deeply as she studied the photos on his documents. She held the license and passport up to more easily compare the photos to the face. Her eyes flicked back and forth several times.

"This one sort of looks like you and this one doesn't at all." She passed all the paperwork back under the ornate screen.

Henry waited a moment, but that seemed to be that. His stomach lurched. He asked to speak to a supervisor. The teller excused herself and disappeared into a back office. Another customer came into the lobby and nodded to Henry as he stepped into what would be a line if there were one. Henry nodded back and faced the window to wait, concentrating on his breathing and trying not to let his guts tighten up. He hated not having any credit cards, club memberships or even a library card. He hated feeling like a non-person.

"Mr. Stillwater?" A smooth-faced, crew-cut-haired man in a shirt and tie who looked to be about eighteen years old opened a door to the right of the row of tellers' windows. "Come on back." He waited for Henry to come around and closed the door behind them. "Cash." They shook hands. "My name is Cash. Mom is a huge fan of the man in black. She hasn't noticed the relevance to banking yet." Henry sat across from Cash in a tidy office with a basketball hoop over the door and a photo of a smiling young woman hugging a smiling golden retriever on the desk.

"Sorry about Frau Blucher out there, she takes her job way too seriously. I guess she's more of a Nurse Ratched. Let's see your stuff, I'll get you set up." Cash keyed a few entries in his computer. "And welcome to Skagway. Dyea is the best spot to be in. Town is cool, but Dyea is calm and quiet, awesome hiking, skiing. You can skate when it gets a little colder, raft the river in summer . . . okay, I activated your card . . . and here's your balance." Cash swiveled his computer monitor around to where Henry could see it.

Henry couldn't believe his eyes. He had nearly eighteen hundred dollars. "Um, there must be a mistake. That's more than I . . ."

"Well, let's look. You've got a deposit from Social Security and one other check deposit from a law firm. I spoke, or rather listened, to your lawyer on the phone. She called last week. Very persuasive woman. Looks like you are new to social security this year since your birthdate is . . . oh hey, February 29. How cool is that? Well, she got your payments started already. Anyway, after her call I got an email from someone way, way up-line urging me to make sure you have everything you need. Does your attorney play golf? So, you can see here, you'll be getting twelve hundred and thirty dollars a month and you can expect that the third Wednesday each month. You're in the Weinstien place with no mortgage, no utilities and unless you have a debilitating drug habit or set up a high stakes poker game, which I hope you will since I'd be there in a heartbeat, you should be able to manage on that. Of course, you can get a summer job and earn up to fifteen grand without penalty." Cash smiled and rocked back in his chair. "That's a great property. I've been to a couple keggers there. If you ever want to sell, I'd consider it a huge personal favor to hear about it first. Anything else I can do for you today? Like the letter said, you have basically a checking and a savings account, so you'll want to apportion your funds. Maybe you want to think about that. Order some checks. Like anyone uses checks anymore. Our ATM works pretty well except on the really busy ship days."

Henry shook Cash's hand again and walked out. The shopping list in his head began to bloom and re-prioritize itself. There would be more protein in his life. As he left the bank he visited the ATM in the entry. He used his new card and his new PIN to withdraw cash. It felt so good he didn't even mind the fee. He'd been very nervous carrying the five hundred dollars in cash he left Texas with. He couldn't afford to lose it. Each expenditure cut into it, eroding his net worth. He'd started with bus and ferry tickets paid for, but had to buy a room in Bellingham and food for the whole trip. He picked up discarded sections of newspapers and read old magazines. He was down to seventy-three dollars this morning. In the back of his mind he'd considered what would happen if something had gone wrong with his social security or if A. J. had not sent what was left after his final settlement. Or if he owed more. The consideration had not led to any action plans. He had no idea what he would do. Maybe he could have sold what was left of his Zoloft. That was probably a parole violation.

At the post office, Henry was third in line. First was a very old woman about four feet tall trying to pick from a selection of first class stamps. When she finally narrowed it to Carmen Miranda or Lunar Landings, the elderly man behind her said, "Oh for Chrissake, Genevieve, take some of both."

The short woman shuffled around in a pivot and lifted the bones of her face upward, leaving the wrinkles draped around her neck. "Oh, it's you, you old buzzard. How've you been?" They chatted for a few minutes. She rotated back to the counter and resumed her business. She asked for half a sheet of each. The clerk carefully halved the sheets, tucked the stamps in an enveloped and finished the sale. When Henry's turn came there were several people behind him, all visiting amiably. He left the counter with nothing from general delivery and all the people in line were quiet while he walked to the mailbox room. He heard conversation resume when he rounded the corner.

Box thirty-two was a large one on the bottom row. Henry used the pink ribbon key and opened the door. He carefully stowed several letters and bills and two flat packages in the tote bag without reading any names and slid the bundle inside his pack. He made sure to zip it closed. Next stop was the bookstore for newspapers and an Alaska map. In place of Minerva, a young woman about Esme's age with four hair braids extending from a Rasta cap to her waist offered him Monday and Tuesday's *Wall Street Journals* as soon as he'd said hello. He asked about local papers and maps and the woman offered the *Juneau Empire* and the more local *Skagway News*. He took both. She directed him to the back of the store to a map display.

Henry drove slowly around the blocks both gas stations sat on. One was clearly newer, but that wouldn't mean anything to Ms. Walton. He parked on the street and watched a few customers at the older one. He did the same at the newer one. Neither one struck him as safer. He flipped a coin.

The grocery store was colorful and noisy. Several people clogged each aisle, leaning over carts in animated visiting as much as shopping. Henry kept his head down and eyes on the task at hand until he reached for the last package of ten-inch flour tortillas. Another hand was on the package, a hand with long fingers and several rings. He made eye contact with Minerva.

"Mr. Stillwater."

"Ms. Black." He let go of the package.

"You've gotta get here sooner for some things, they go quickly. Then it's another week. Not willing to fight for these?" She raised an eyebrow, held up and waggled the package.

"No, ma'am. I can do with these." He grabbed the last pack of burrito-size tortillas.

"Too bad. Everyone gets into the occasional scuffle over particular items. I would have fought for these today. I'm making chicken enchiladas for the potluck Sunday and these are the only size that fit my dish. You're coming, right?"

"Excuse me?"

"To church. We share a meal afterward this week. It's the best food you'll get around here. I heard someone was bringing Swedish meatballs and that there may be rhubarb merengue pie. Ms. Walton always brings killer deviled eggs or cream puffs. I'm hoping for cream puffs. God, I hope no one buys all the cream before she gets here. What's your dish?"

Henry thought. "I don't have a dish. And I haven't been invited."

"I'm inviting you, for Pete's sake. Bachelors, such as yourself, especially ones with simple kitchens as in no refrigeration or a Cuisinart, are held to a simpler standard of potluck dishes. Some of your neighbors crank out spectacular stuff with little gadgetry, but they all have electricity now. You could get away with a dip or a cheese and cracker plate. Maybe even just olives and pickles. Be careful with pickles, though, several people make their own and they're awesome." Minerva smiled. "Good luck."

How am I going to get out of this, Henry asked himself. To Minerva, he said, "We'll see how it goes." He let the large tortillas drop into his cart. As soon as the plastic smacked the bottom of the cart, he heard a groan and a whispered "dammit" behind him. He turned but couldn't tell who was miffed that he got the last package of any size tortillas. Henry shopped on, selecting peanut butter, Greek yogurt, spaghetti sauce, eggs, cheese, cans of black beans, diced tomatoes and green chiles. His goal was enough food for at least a week of fresh things and stuff like cans, crackers and pasta for long term. Meat and vegetables would be a challenge until he learned better how to keep them. The old wood box on the outside of the cabin was a reliable refrigerator or freezer, depending on the temperature. It had heavy wire mesh to keep rodents out, he assumed. Henry found Spam, chipped beef, potted meat and jerky, but passed it by several times before picking out a few cans of tuna and salmon. Lunch in prison was commonly canned ham or breaded fried Spam covered with gravy. One of his fellow inmates loved the chicken-fried Spam and traded for more of it. The memory of it made Henry's stomach squirm.

He ran into Minerva again in paper goods. She asked if he got the *Wall Street Journals* she saved for him.

"Yes, thank you. I got a Juneau paper and the local one, too."

"Be sure to read the wall in the entry here at the store and at the post office for local events. I hear someone in Dyea is planning a yard sale this weekend. A moving sale, actually, could be big. Hardly any lettuce left, you should get back over to produce." Minerva dodged carts on her way to check-out.

Henry had everything on his list and plenty of food for someone who isn't fussy or very creative. He asked a woman stocking shelves in paper goods where to find stationery supplies. She showed him her small selection and told him to go to the hardware store for more. At the check-out counter, Henry debated whether to use his new debit card or cash. He watched two people ahead of him use cards and get cash back, too. He could have gotten cash without a fee. He decided not to use his card yet. Since he made the deal with Darwin for free firewood, he didn't need a lot of cash. After putting the groceries in the back of the car, he checked the time and walked to Broadway to the hardware store.

The little Maryland town Henry spent most of his growing up years in had a hardware store like this one. The floors were wood and rose and fell to different parts of the old building. Two old men in the fishing gear aisle argued at high volume over when to start going out for kings. Henry thought all the salmon fishing was later in the year, so listened in while selecting extra batteries for his flashlight. He decided to get a second flashlight for backup. He found the stationery aisle and picked up a pad of lined paper and one of unlined. The five-pack of pencils was the best deal. He looked at sharpeners, but remembered his pocketknife and thought that would do as well. He liked pencils and had used fancy mechanical ones since . . . he couldn't even remember when. Did he need envelopes? He couldn't think of anything he'd need one for, but better safe than sorry. There were party supplies, too; things like birthday candles and packages of themed invitations, plates and decorations. He took a pack of plain thumbtacks for hanging up his new Alaska Map E, the most detailed one the bookstore had.

Out on the boardwalk again, Henry watched as two people on bicycles met and visited in the middle of the street and he realized his face didn't hurt. There was no wind. Skagway was a pleasure to walk around without having to deal with wind. He went to the end of Congress Way and looked at the dock and small boat harbor. The water was low and the ramps to the floats were at about a forty-five degree slant. The air smelled like a beach. On the way back into town, Henry stopped to watch a snowflake take its sweet time in coming to earth. It was his first since the last ski trip he'd taken with Claire. Henry shivered and headed for the library. The one flake was followed by a few thousand more, aimless little bits that disappeared when they hit the ground.

Esme was already at the library doing her homework when Henry got there. She showed him around and introduced him to the librarian who suggested they use the small meeting room with a whiteboard. They settled in and went to work. Any nerves Henry felt about trying to help Esme quickly turned to positive energy. She listened, asked questions, tried hard to understand and was a real pleasure to work with. Very quickly Henry was convinced there was nothing wrong with her brain, it just worked a little differently than her textbook did. He'd seen that over and over with people he hired and people he worked with. Everyone's head works a little differently. Having patience with that and then taking advantage of it was one of his biggest business advantages.

"Thanks for doing this," Esme said. "I was starting to think I was retarded. If you could go over the homework with me a couple more times, I think I'll be okay. Like maybe the next two weeks?"

"Sure. Do you want to plan on Wednesdays?"

"Yeah, that works for me. Darwin said he talked to you about his speech. I'm just glad he's thinking about it. He's at my house now, using my computer. Are you staying? You could check your email."

"Oh. I guess I could." Henry hadn't checked his email since he got out of prison. He kept in touch with Jason for the case and then the release. He couldn't think of anyone to write to. "More likely I'll find something to read."

Esme put on her coat and picked up her bag to put her book away. "Oh, here are some cookies my mom sent you." She handed over a brown paper lunch bag and left. Henry carefully opened the bag to look inside. He smelled cinnamon and saw about a dozen large snickerdoodles. He wondered what Esme's mom thought of a stranger, a convict, tutoring her daughter. He glanced up to make sure no one was in view of the door and stuffed a cookie in his mouth. His eyes closed and he was transported back to Maryland and the warm cookies and cold milk that waited for him to come home from school. His mother made snickerdoodles often.

Henry thanked the librarian for his new library card and walked through swirling snow to the grocery store. There were full tote bags in a very tidy row next to his plastic sacked food, so the plan with Ms. Walton was on schedule. He drove to the church and parked within view of the door, leaving the motor running. Ms. Walton was right on time and in a very good mood.

"Oh, don't you just love snow?" She hummed a particular melody over and over and snowflakes played with the headlights all the way home. Their driveways had about two inches of snow on them.

## NITA NETTLETON

# 8

Snow was still coming down in the morning. Henry started out the door to the outhouse in the cabin slippers, but went back for his new second-hand tall rubber boots. He waded through about a foot of light, fluffy snow. Back in the cabin he cranked up the radio and listened to the news. The weather report described a combo of a high over the land keeping the temperature down and a low over the water dumping snow. Henry bathed and ate before gathering his laundry. He considered that he should have gotten a basket or something to put laundry in. He settled for a Panther duffel bag he'd found under the dresser. By the time he dressed for going out and got the snow shovel from the woodshed, there was another six inches. He cleared and swept around his doorways and made a path to the outhouse. Next he shoveled a space in front of the woodshed and carried two armloads of wood into the house. The temperature held at about twenty-five degrees. He decided to take the shovel to Ms. Walton's and clear her walkways.

Snow piled up against Henry's knees on the silent slog to Ms. Walton's. Now and then huge clumps of it fell down with a delicate whump from tree branches. The forest had a very different look. It had been a considerable number of years since Henry had been anywhere around such deep, powdery snow, let alone walked through it. He slung his bag over his shoulder and shoveled the last fifteen feet to Ms. Walton's garage. He cleared out an area about four feet wide in front of the garage door, then shoveled to the front steps, up the steps and around the side of the house to the kitchen door. By the time he straightened up at her steps, he felt a slow burn in the muscles in his shoulders and back. They were the same muscles that hurt after Monday and Tuesday's work with Darwin. He rapped gently on the door, waited a moment listening, then opened the door and peeked inside. He smelled something yeasty baking and heard soft piano music.

There was a broom inside the door. Henry used it to brush off his pants, the doorway and the steps. He pulled his boots off and set them on a rug inside the door. He neither saw nor heard Ms. Walton, so followed her previous instruction to start his laundry. He left the settings as they were for cold water and medium size. He didn't have a lot, just underwear, t-shirts, socks, handkerchiefs, his pillow cases, two shirts, and a pair of jeans. He closed the washer lid and turned to put his boots back on, but jumped when the piano music soared and Ms. Walton belted out "Ex-sul-ta-te, Ju-bi-la-te!" She went on with several lines in Latin, apparently repeated, her voice rising and falling.

Taking the broom, Henry slipped into his boots and went outside. He cleaned the front steps and made a path to the small woodshed to the west of the house. The shovel clunked onto something solid like stone beside the shed and he fished around in the snow to find the edges of it. The piled snow fell away and he could see a head figure. It was about two feet high, very stout and looked like a man with long hair and a beard. Definitely Biblical. He cleaned carefully around it and worked his way back to the garage, clearing the snow further back and piling it between the trees. The quiet snowfall made the sounds of the house easy to hear. The washing machine drained and refilled to rinse. The piano approached and went through the same piece several times and Ms. Walton sang.

Henry packed his clean, wet laundry back into the duffel, carefully swept out the entry, replaced the broom, and closed the door behind him. There was another three inches of snow where he had cleared in front of the garage. He could barely see his own buried footprints on the driveway in the flat light. He hung up his wet things at home, draping over chairs, the sofa back, the dresser, bookcase and woodpile next to the wood stove. He could feel a spike in the humidity in the cabin and it felt good. He had gotten a can of cocoa mix at the store and heated water for a cup while he spread out newspapers.

After refolding and chucking his third *Wall Street Journal* into the kindling box, Henry concluded the thrill was gone. It took only the three issues after a long abstinence to get caught up on world news and to meet new players in the financial sphere. He was pleased the stock market was doing well, but now that he was not involved in it, felt no thrill. Nothing on the financial pages seemed all that important. He ate a snickerdoodle and opened *The Skagway News*. The local paper covered a period of two weeks in twelve tabloid pages. Henry learned the joys and agonies of the Panther basketball teams, boys and girls, the robotics team's stellar performance and travel plans to attend the state meet, and about a girl in Dyea who was mowing her way through all regional competition in archery. She traveled and competed in person, but also competed via video with archers throughout Southeast Alaska. A dog named Tuffy, missing for days in Skagway, was found, hungry but unharmed, trapped under someone's house. A neighbor had heard howling, but thought it was the wind. She wouldn't have forgiven herself, "If...you know." The Skagway Borough Assembly revisited the rules on urban barnyard fowl. Mushroom farming was lauded as a promising growth industry in Haines, now supporting several families. Henry asked his cocoa mug, "Who wouldn't find all this more engrossing than who should have done what in Syria?"

The snowfall diminished to the occasional, half-hearted flake after Henry flipped his drying clothes over, swept the floor, re-shoveled the path to the outhouse and had a nap. It had completely stopped and there was a low fog cloaking the heavily laden trees when he went out to check the temperature. Low twenties. He stretched his arms over his head and twisted his back side-to-side a few times. The muscles were a little sore, nothing big. The muffled white landscape reminded him of something. He inhaled damp air and concentrated. His second year in college, a big snow shut everything down and Ellen Dieffenbacher – his eyes flew open. A car horn was beeping over at Ms. Walton's. Not automatically like a car alarm, but someone was pushing the horn repeatedly like they needed help. Henry jumped into his boots, grabbed his coat, hat and gloves off the peg by the door and hurried as fast as he could go through the deep snow.

Ms. Walton's garage door was open and her front door was ajar. Henry ran up the steps and nudged open the door. Inside, Ms. Walton knelt next to a small, blanketed pile on her living room floor.

"Hal, thank God. I need you to come here and hold him." She scooted around to give Henry room to kneel next to her and put his hands on the small heap. "I'll be right back. Don't let him get up." She got up and ran up the stairs. Henry could see a small nose shaking beneath the edge of the blanket. He shifted his hands and settled into a more comfortable position and heard a piteous little moan. He began cooing a reassuring stream of "there, there," hoping whatever was in the blanket would hold still. He could feel the rise and fall of breathing with a shudder each breath. He added a few, "now, nows." Ms. Walton slid to a stop on her knees next to him with a basket full of medical supplies. She quickly put on a pair of latex gloves.

## Nowhere Else To Go, but Dyea

She lifted the edge of the blanket, slid in her hand and cooed reassuring variations on "There's a good boy, it's okay now." Another piteous moan escaped the blanket. She looked at Henry and said, "I don't think anything's broken. You pick him up and follow me. We need to get him on the kitchen table." Before he could ask what "he" was, she was on her feet and headed to the kitchen. Henry scooped up the little bundle as carefully as he could and followed. At the kitchen table, Ms. Walton swept the top with her arm and knocked the napkin holder, matching salt and peppers and several bread pans to the floor. "Right here," she ordered, "and keep him still." After stripping off her gloves, she turned the water on at the sink and slid up the sleeves of her sweater. She washed her hands and came back with a dishpan of hot water. "Now, pull back the blanket and we'll get started." Henry did as she said and gently pulled back the edge of the blanket. What caught his eye first was all the blood. Several open gashes crossed the legs and rib cage of a small white dog, maybe a corgi mix. "Try laying your hand across his face, cover his eyes and hold his head." Henry forgot he was still wearing gloves. He pulled them off quickly and laid his right across the little dog's face, his thumb down the back of the neck. Ms. Walton re-gloved, pulled a few things out of the basket and began cleaning the wounds with gauze. She threaded a curved needle and sewed up the long gashes. The little dog shook the entire time, but otherwise held still. Next came alcohol swabs along all the suture lines and wrapped dressings. A tiny pink tongue licked Henry's fingers.

Ms. Walton dumped out the contents of a laundry basket and lay a clean folded blanket in the bottom. She filled several jars with warm water, screwed on the lids and buried them in the blanket. She peeled back the top layer. "Okay, Hal, let's put little Albedo in here." He lifted the dog and lay him on the clean blanket. Ms. Walton covered him up to his neck. She carried the basket to the living room and settled in a wing chair, rocking and shushing. Henry washed the blood off his hands, took off his coat and slipped off his boots to set by the back door. He picked up bloody clumps of gauze and put them in the trash can in the corner. He dumped the dishpan, filled it part way with soapy water, added a little bleach from the jug in the laundry room and used a sponge from the back of the sink to clean the table. He set the bloody blanket on top of the washing machine and put the napkin holder, salt, pepper, and bread pans back on the clean table. He carried the dishpan into the living room and wiped up the blood on the hardwood floor. Ms. Walton was fully engrossed in rocking Albedo. Henry washed out the dishpan and sponge with more bleach, leaving them in the sink. He retrieved his boots, gloves and coat and tiptoed back to set them by the front door. He didn't know if he were still needed, but hadn't been dismissed, so he sat on the sofa.

"He lost a lot of blood, but may be okay. Poor little thing. Some kind of vicious bites. I'll give him antibiotics if he lives through the night." Ms. Walton closed her eyes, kept rocking and hummed a lullaby. After a few minutes she stopped and peeked under the blanket. "He's sleeping," she whispered. "His pulse is not bad." Easing the basket into the chair beside her, Ms. Walton fixed her eyes on Henry. "Our concern now is Squint. If he is able, he'll be looking for Albedo. You need to go find him. He lives right up the hill from here, but it's a cliff and he goes around from West Creek somewhere. There are snowshoes in the garage." She closed her eyes and started the lullaby again.

In the garage, Henry found the snowshoes. They were fairly modern with plastic bindings and aluminum frames. He carried them outside the door and took a few moments to figure out how to put them on. The hike back to his house was much easier with them on. He put on the insulated coveralls and flap hat, put a water bottle, both flashlights, extra hat and gloves in his pockets and headed out to the main road. There was no sound, hardly any light and mounded heaps of white under the trees and across the roadway. Someone had driven through the snowfall at some point leaving the suggestion of tracks in the middle of the road. Henry turned left to go to West Creek. He hadn't worn snowshoes in about forty-five years, he figured, but found a workable stride pretty quickly. He started with a flashlight on, but turned it off when he got on the road. It was easier to see without it. It took about twice as long to get to the West Creek bridge as it had before all the snow. He crossed the bridge and turned left. A small fork presented itself and he remembered Darwin had taken the right fork to go up the hill for woodcutting. Henry could see a light up the left fork. He went that way and made a few turns in the drive before seeing a porch light. As he got closer, a Gambrel-roofed house took shape. The house was dark except for the porch light and a glow behind curtains from the front room. He stomped a few steps back and forth in the deep snow in front of the porch. He knocked.

A woman wrapped in a blanket and holding a book opened the door. "Oh! Where did you come from? Come in!" She stepped back.

"That's okay, ma'am, I don't want to take these things off. Sorry to bother you, but I'm looking for Squint. Do you know where he lives?"

"Yes," she said, "you can go up West Creek Road and over the new bridge back along the hill, that's the way I think he takes his bike, but it's quicker to go up the Lost Lake Trail. No way you'd get up there in the snow. You didn't drive here, did you?"

"No, I walked from my place. Next door to Ms. Walton."

"Oh, you're the new guy. You sure you won't come in? It's not a real good time to go looking for Squint."

"His dog is injured and Ms. Walton thought he'd be looking for him."

"Albedo? What happened?"

"Some kind of bites, ma'am."

"Oh my God! Well, you're not going to find Squint out in this."

"Doesn't sound like it. Thank you, sorry to disturb you."

"Not at all and be sure to come back sometime. Come meet the family. The highway is closed and everyone's stuck in Whitehorse. In fact, come over Saturday. We're having a barbecue. I guess now it'll be a snow-be-cue."

"Yes, ma'am, thank you." Henry hiked back to the fork in the road. He didn't know where to try next. Up the road seemed sensible, but surely Squint wouldn't be trying to ride his bike in the snow. And Henry had no idea where the Lost Lake trail was. It seemed doubtful he could even follow a trail with all the snow and the dark. He turned to head for home. On the other side of the West Creek bridge, he saw a light bobbing in the road. When the light got closer, he heard a female voice.

"Hello! Squint?"

Henry met a small woman on skis with a headlamp. "No, I'm Henry. I'm looking for Squint."

"Oh, I'm Ruby. I just saw him a bit ago on snowshoes, so I was surprised to see him again. But he's not you. Henry, did you say? Wait, I know you."

Now that they were closer, Henry could see long braids under the headlamp. It was the girl he'd seen at the bookstore. "Yes, I live just over there." Henry gestured with his arm. "Which way was he going, I need to find him."

"That way." She pointed toward Henry's house. "He was looking for Albedo, have you seen him?"

"Yes, he's been hurt. Ms. Walton is taking care of him. Was Squint okay?"

"Um, yeah, but he said his camp was a mess. Bunch of snow slid into it and while he was dealing with it, Albedo disappeared. I was looking for my dog, Buttercup. She took off barking. I worry about her in such deep snow, she's no spring chicken."

"Big yellow dog, one flop ear?"

"Uh-huh."

"She visits me sometimes. But not today."

"She likes your house. If she shows up there, just let her in. Can you believe all this snow? See you at the barbecue Saturday." Ruby pushed off and was gone.

Henry followed his own tracks back to the turn-off and had to work a lot less than he did breaking trail. He turned up Ms. Walton's drive to report his failure to find Squint. On her porch he saw a hunched figure put on snowshoes, then sling what looked like a bag full of toys onto his back. The figure turned and hopped down the steps, landing lightly and straightening up. A grizzled head with one wide eye and one slitted squinty one popped out from under a hood about five feet in front of Henry.

"Yo, pardner," Squint rasped, "scared the bejeezus out of me!" He stepped aside to go around Henry, but stopped. "You're the fella was driving Lily the other day, bless you."

It took Henry a moment to realize he was referring to Ms. Walton. Interesting. "Name's Henry. How's Albedo?"

"Well, he gave me a scare, merciful Heaven, but doesn't look too bad, no. He was smart to come here. You staying here?"

"Um, no, I'm over there." Henry pointed over his shoulder with his thumb.

"Me, too. Let's go, brother, I'm freezing." He headed off, tramping quietly through the snow. Henry turned and followed. At the end of Henry's porch, they stopped and began taking off snowshoes. Henry had his head down and was surprised by a big wet dog tongue on his cheek.

"Serious!" He reached up and rubbed her head. "Or should I say, Buttercup?" She wagged her tail and hobbled to stand by the door. Squint got there first and opened it. He fished in his pocket for a lighter and lit the small candle inside. Henry followed and they both took off coats, hats and gloves. Both chucked their boots. Henry lit the lamp on the table. He could see Serious Buttercup was already sprawled on the rug. In the growing light, he saw dark patches on her forelegs and chest. He squatted next to her and saw more on her face. It looked like blood. There were no wounds on her that he could see. He concluded it was someone else's blood. She was clearly exhausted. Squint had hauled his lumpy sack to a corner and after opening the damper on the stove and putting in two logs, closing the damper again and adjusting a small draft control on the back of the stove, he sank down on the couch.

"Looks like you've made yourself to home here, Henry. You gotta watch that draft, she'll hold better now, yep. I'm all in." Squint's eyes drooped and he began snoring. Henry felt all in, too, but didn't feel quite comfortable with all this company in the house. He ate some yogurt and a spoonful of peanut butter, washed down two Aleve with about a quart of water and read a few items in the Juneau paper. His eyes drooped. Neither dog nor forest elf had moved. Both snored. Henry went to bed.

# 9

Henry woke to the smell of coffee. He lay still and listened. He heard the door open and close and some raspy whispers. There was enough daylight to make his way around the house, but just barely. He had slept in his long underwear so put on slippers and his fleece jacket. Following the coffee smell to the kitchen, he got a mug off the shelf and poured. Sipping, he surveyed the cabin. Serious Buttercup lay on the rug, deliberately scrubbing her forelegs with her tongue. Squint sat cross-legged on the floor next to her, bent over a sketch pad, drawing and muttering. He had a steaming coffee cup balanced on one knee.

"Good coffee," Henry offered quietly, hoping not to disturb the pastoral rustic scene in his living room. Both roommates turned to look at him. One with a one-eyed blink, the other with a tail flip. "Burritos for breakfast?" No one responded. "Maybe in a bit, then." He dipped a pan of warm water from the pot on the wood stove, got a small towel and settled down next to Serious Buttercup. "Let me help you with that." She held up her chin while he washed her face and neck, massaging the dried blood out of her fur. He wanted to make sure she wasn't injured and examined what he could reach of her body. She rolled onto her side and lifted her hind leg to expose her belly. He gave it a rub. She had one red, swollen spot on a forefoot pad and a small welt at the end of one ear, but nothing else. Henry got a tube of Neosporin from his dresser top and dabbed some on her ear and foot and finished cleaning up her legs. She yawned and fell asleep.

Squint said, "She went out to pee, yep, looked around and listened. All quiet now." He took a drink of his coffee and straightened his legs out on the floor. "Here's what I think happened." He held up the drawing. It was a swirl of pastel blue froth with a four-legged demon leaping after a four-legged cherub with wings. Below was a four-legged Madonna, reaching up as though to catch the cherub. In the lower corner was a half demon, half angel woman figure holding a bundle in her arms. Squint waited, then looked at the drawing. "See, this is the coyote come to steal our leftover stew, yep, and this is Albedo trying to defend it. The snow let go in an avalanche and they both tumbled down the cliff, merciful Heaven. Buttercup caught Albedo, killed the coyote and then she broke trail to lead Albedo to salvation at Lily's house. She was an ER nurse, yep. But she's pitiful blind more than ten feet out and thought Buttercup was a wolf and launched a hail of rocks. Then she heard Albedo calling to her and took him in, yep." He drained his coffee cup. "I was busy packing up when our tent collapsed, but saw the coyote dart in and Albedo take after it. They disappeared over the side. I gathered up what I could and worked my way down. Lord, that was a task, and heard the most awful sounds, but when I got to the bottom all that was there was the dead coyote, sent back to Hell. And blood. But the snow covered the trail too quick and I was confused for a time, Lord. Buttercup came and got me, yep." He stroked her head. She snored.

"Well." Henry got the coffee pot and filled Squint's cup as well as his own before sitting at the table. He noticed Squint's lumpy sack in the corner was replaced with a rolled sleeping bag, a very tidy stack of art paper pads and prepaid mailers, charcoal and pencils, oil pastels, and a stack of books. Tucked against the books was a little tower of brown paper wrapped packages. In front of the packages was a bag of Raven's Brew Deadman's Reach coffee in a small cooking pot. "Mind if I turn on the radio and catch the news?"

"Mm. If we get any more snow, we'll want to shovel off the roof over the bedroom." Squint stood and stretched, carried his boots to the back door and went out. Henry checked the temperature on the front porch and peed off the end away from the steps. After cranking up the radio he washed his hands and face and got out tortillas, canned beans, cheese, jalapenos and eggs. He put three huge tortillas on top of the wood stove to warm and put the beans in a pan on the cook stove. Guessing Buttercup wouldn't want hot peppers, he didn't add them to the beans. He had only two plates. Ms. Walton's pie tin hadn't been returned yet, so he designated that as Buttercup's dish. He thought of water for her and found a bowl with mutant ninja turtles printed on it to fill and set by the door.

Squint stomped at the back door and carried his boots through to the front door. "That's a fine book you've got in the outhouse, yep. I'd heard about it, but not seen it before." He peered into the pot on the wood stove. "Good idea. I didn't have to wash up in the snow." He sat down on the couch. "I'll give Albedo another hour before I go over, Lily is not an early riser, no."

Both men listened to a news report about the snow. It was over for now, but could come again over the weekend. There was a phone interview with someone from the Log Cabin Ski Society in Skagway saying a crew was headed up to work on trails as soon as the highway opened. It would take a lot of work to be ready for the ski race in two weeks. Henry remembered reading about it in the local paper. There would be a new award category this year for the best theme costumes and the theme was Babes in the Woods. He got up to stir the beans and flip the tortillas. "You want jalapenos in your burrito?"

"Yes, sir. And..." Squint scrambled down to his pile of belongings and sorted through the brown paper packages. "Here's cumin, cayenne and cilantro, if you wish, brother. Go easy on the cumin, but you can't overdo cilantro, no."

Henry took the packages. "Does Buttercup like spicy?" Squint shrugged. Henry put one of the warm tortillas on the pie plate and scooped out her share of the beans before seasoning the rest and setting the pot to simmer. He scrambled eggs and poured them in a hot skillet with olive oil, quickly sliced cheese and put several pieces on Buttercup's beans. When the eggs solidified, he put a spoonful over her cheese before folding it all up and setting her plate by the door next to her bowl of water. She had been watching since the beans warmed to smelliness. She got up, plodded over and dug in. Henry fixed two plates and carried them to the table. Squint pumped water to fill two glasses and sat down. He bowed his head and mumbled a prayer before picking up his fork.

Over breakfast, Henry learned what he should be doing with his garbage when the bears wake up and that, if he were sticking around awhile, he should start composting and get his garden going. He hadn't thought about gardening, but liked the idea. With the price of vegetables and how far away the store was, maybe he should grow a few things. How hard can it be? He learned that Squint used the house when the weather was bad. Usually, no more than a day or two and for the last few years. The kids rarely came out in deep snow or during big storms, so no conflict. Buttercup and Albedo were good friends.

With rest, food and more conversation, Squint settled down and seemed a little less squirrelly. His camp was a mess now and it would take a bit to fix it.

## Nowhere Else To Go, but Dyea

"No hurry," Henry said. "Maybe I can help you rebuild your camp."

"That would be neighborly of you, brother." Squint filled the empty bean pot with warm water and began washing dishes. "We should eat the stew for supper today. Unless you're Catholic." Henry got dressed and put away his dried laundry. Squint swept the floor. Without discussion, they dressed to go outside. Henry took the clean pie plate to return and his snow shovel to tidy up Ms. Walton's. He wondered if anyone but Squint called her Lily. Buttercup waded off through the snow toward the main road. Her trail behind the woodshed was deeply buried. Squint set a brisk pace in his snowshoes, making Henry struggle to keep up. At Ms. Walton's, Squint went inside with the pie plate and Henry went to work shoveling. The snow level was a little lower than he expected, but the snow itself was denser. He'd heard about how snow settles, but never really seen it. It was actually easier to shovel; sticking together and not whirling around. He cleared all around the house and garage and out further in front than he had before. That's where he ran into half a dozen palm-sized rocks. He remembered Squint's report of her "launching a hail of rocks" and gathered them up to reload the ammo bucket beside the front door. When he finished shoveling, he sat on the porch to rest. A light but spirited piano piece began in the house. He listened to the whole thing.

Just as Henry stood and stretched, ready to go home, Squint came out the door with a bundle in his arms. He gently handed it to Henry to hold while he put on his snowshoes. It wasn't heavy enough to be Albedo. Henry peeked under the dish towel wrapper and smelled before he saw two golden brown loaves of fresh bread. Squint stood up and saw the look on his face. He smiled and reached into his pocket and showed the top of a jar of something purple and homemade. Squint said no more until they got back to the cabin and unwrapped the bread and jar of blueberry jam.

"Albedo is better today, but needs quiet rest. Lily wants to watch him for a few days to make sure the antibiotics work for him. And so." Squint wandered around the room, not quite but almost pacing.

"I thought I'd go work in the woodshed, if you want to help," Henry said. They began putting gear back on. "What was that piano piece I heard at Ms. Walton's?"

"Mm, yes, that was Handel, "Let the Bright Seraphim"! She's working on the choral arrangement for Easter. Bold, that woman, very bold."

The first order of business in the woodshed was shoveling out enough room to work. As soon as Henry dug out the splitting block, Squint picked up the maul and began wailing. Henry thought to suggest they use Darwin's power splitter hunkered under the snow around the corner, but couldn't get a word in edgewise. Squint told the story of his life while he sent firewood flying and Henry scrambled to gather and stack it. The story didn't cover his whole life, just the last twenty-five years. He began with killing his wife, then described twenty years as a fugitive working for a tiny room and nothing else in a catacomb-like used bookstore in Tonopah, Nevada. There he found a nineteen-year-old newspaper someone had used to wrap a rare book and read that his wife was not dead. The news story was about her winning a Power Ball. She described herself as a widow. After that, Squint drifted west and came to Dyea. He had studied many things in the bookstore, including Latin, Esperanto, drawing, and painting, but focused on fungi and climate science. He was convinced that humans were doomed and would take the rest of life on Earth with them, but for the Fungus Kingdom. Fungi were plotting now how to sterilize all humans, as well as their pets and livestock, to stop them in their destructive path without actually hurting anyone. "Fungi are quite benevolent," he concluded.

## Nowhere Else To Go, but Dyea

By dusk all the wood was split and stacked. Henry took an Aleve midday and offered the bottle to Squint. With a quiet, "Hallelujah," he took one. They warmed up the stew Squint had stashed in the fridge/freezer and sliced fresh bread to eat with it. Henry had almost passed on butter at the store since he hadn't bought bread, but thought he'd want it for other things. He couldn't think now what that would have been, but was glad he got it for Ms. Walton's bread. The stew had more than one kind of mushroom in it and was delicious.

"Where do you find mushrooms?" Henry asked, slicing more bread.

"I picked these in July and dried them. There is some lichen in here, too. One of the reasons I stay here is for the lichen. That and studying the toads." He looked up at Henry. "No toads in the stew, no. Only squirrel."

After they ate and cleaned up, Henry revisited his Juneau paper and Squint painted. He showed Henry a finely detailed piece he was working on with angels leading children through a mine field. "I illustrate what Sister Mary Reginald sends me. She writes the children's books, I do the illustrations. I don't think the other Daughters of St. Paul know about me. She pays me cash. None of my business, the rest of it, no."

After breakfast the next morning, they heard a low rumbling. Out between the trees along the driveway they could see Darwin's truck with a plow on the front slowly working back and forth, snow flying ahead of him. He worked his way into the yard and cleared a central area, then worked to push snow back to either side in huge berms. He carefully cleared easy access to the woodshed and exhumed his wood splitter. When he was finished he had plenty of room to turn around and parked the truck backed up to the splitter. He met Buttercup halfway across the yard and they came in the cabin together.

"Hey, Squid Face, how's things?" Darwin took the cup of coffee Henry handed him.

"Can't complain, Dog Breath." Squint smiled up at Darwin from his spot on the floor with his painting.

"Someone did a hell of a job in that woodshed. Saved me firing up the damn splitter. And now I don't have to put gas in it. Guy in town wants to buy it. Hey, is that Ms. Walton's bread?" He helped himself to a sawed-off chunk.

"There's butter and blueberry jam," Henry suggested. "Don't you need the splitter?"

Darwin smeared a huge glob of butter across half the bread slab and topped it with jam before folding it over. "Now we're talking." He took a big bite. When he could speak, he continued. "Not that piece of shit. Woman in Tagish has a new one she wants to sell. Her husband left her in January, she's selling off all his stuff cheap in case he decides to come back. She's even got the paperwork. Hank, this is clearly better coffee than you buy."

"Yeah, it's Squint's. You been to Ms. Walton's yet?" Henry wanted to return her snowshoes as soon as he didn't need them anymore.

"I went there first and was glad to see she was already shoveled out. I guess I have one of you to thank, she never does it. I see all your stuff's here, Squint, have you moved in?"

"Just temporarily. My camp is buried and little Albedo was assailed by a coyote, Lord Almighty. Buttercup saved him and Lily sewed him up. She's holding him for a day or two, the angel of mercy."

"Holy shit! That's a drag. Who's Buttercup?"

"She's the dog also known as Serious," Henry said.

Darwin regarded the comatose yellow hulk on the rug. "Huh." He headed for the door. "Well, I'm going to load up some wood and grab that damn splitter."

## Nowhere Else To Go, but Dyea

Henry slipped into his boots and coat and followed him out, putting gloves on as he walked across the clean white yard. Snow squeaked a little under his boots. They settled into an easy rhythm tossing wood into the back of the truck.

"How do you like old Squint? Kind of a piece of work."

"Frankly, he seems to fit in just fine here. He calls Ms. Walton 'Lily.'"

"I didn't know she had a first name. I wonder what their story is."

"Both good cooks. Did you know about his theory on fungus?" Henry paraphrased what Squint told him.

"Huh." Darwin took a moment to think about it. "Well, your good luck holds with getting a roommate for a few days."

"It's nothing to do with me. My house has a lot of friends. Certainly more friends than I've got."

"A guy can't have too many friends on the one hand, Hank, but all you really need is one. That's what I'm trying to write my essay about, is friendship. But when I get down to putting words together, I don't think I really know anything about it."

Henry paused in his work and faced Darwin. "I've only known you a week and I'd say you know more about friendship than most people."

"Well, maybe. Whatever I know I got from my dad. He never had anything and wound up driving into Long Bay, but his friends still miss him. And he wasn't very good at being a dad. He was more of a friend to me, too, and that's how I miss him."

"Wow. Write that."

"Yeah." They went back to work. "I think Squint and Ms. Walton understand each other. Neither gets along well with other people, but somehow they're on the same page. She lets him play her piano and he takes her berry-picking, stuff like that. Maybe they're friends. I heard him play once while I was stacking her wood. He's really good. I don't know what the hell he lives on, can't just be mushrooms and berries."

"He told me," Henry said. "He works for a nun who writes children's books and pays him to illustrate them. They work through the mail. Ms. Walton's mailbox."

"No shit. Well, I sure learned a lot here today." Darwin checked his load, hitched up the splitter and drove away.

Warmed by the work, Henry had taken off his coat, but shivered as he carried it to the house. The fog was gone and patches of blue sky showed between high cirrus clouds. The temperature was stuck at thirty. Henry reached for the door knob to go inside, but stopped. He heard singing. It was a deep voice, laboring trough a series of scales. Probably not Buttercup, he thought to himself and opened the door.

Buttercup was still very much one with the rug, but Squint had gone through a metamorphosis. He stood at the sink, using Henry's razor. A small towel he was using as a washcloth was draped over the edge of the sink. He'd finished climbing the scales, now dug deep for the low notes. Henry hung up his coat and sat at the table. He began leafing through the local paper, but not really paying attention to it.

Squint finished bathing, dumped his wash water and rinsed out the dishpan. He pumped it full of fresh water and carried it to the stove to refill the enamel pot. After he put the pan away, he walked back toward the window and stood flexing his head around in a circle. He made huffing, throat-clearing sounds and then turned to look at Henry. He stood taller than Henry had seen before and was nearly handsome. His eyes almost matched.

In a voice with a barely noticeable rasp under an eye with a barely noticeable squint, Squint said, "Lily needs a baritone." He put on his outdoor gear and left. Henry sat for a few minutes listening to Buttercup snore. He remembered a guy in prison who had a severe facial tic. He said it started when he was arrested and got worse through his trial. Maybe Squint's hunched posture, distorted eye and damaged voice were self-flagellation. Maybe he was ready to give himself a second chance. Being needed is strong stuff. Henry wondered what his self-flagellation was. He felt fairly normal. Zoloft normal. Well, there was the libido thing. He hadn't had an erection in over two years. He got his journal out to write about it. Clearing a spot on the table, he saw a corner of Squint's drawing of the demon coyote, cherub Albedo and Madonna Buttercup under a newspaper. He pulled it out and studied it, seeing a new detail. There was a tiny arrow piercing the coyote's butt.

## Nita Nettleton

# 10

*The snow was piling deeper and Henry had to work to keep moving forward. He'd dashed out of his dorm in a light jacket to make a coffee run, but couldn't find his car among all the white domes in the parking lot. He gave up and headed back, but now he couldn't find his building in the whirling snow. It was dark, he was cold and had no idea if he were going in the right direction. Ellen Dieffenbacher was in his room studying for a chemistry test. Ellen Dieffenbacher with the tight red corkscrew curls hooked over the backs of her tiny pink ears. He smelled coffee and thought he must be getting close to his building and that Ellen must be making coffee. Where did she get coffee? She's such a resourceful girl. Smart and funny with a Bohemian elegance. He really didn't know what she saw in him, but he was glad she saw whatever it was. And she was singing. Singing in a rich, low voice.*

Henry opened his eyes. It was still dark, but there was a soft light in the main room and he could see a man in his kitchen pouring coffee.

Squint had a candle burning in the corner where he organized his belongings. The sleeping bag was still lying open on the floor, but he had his books and art supplies bagged. He adjusted the damper on the wood stove as Henry shuffled out of the bedroom and filled a coffee cup. "If you are still of a mind to help, you could ease my burden today, brother. Big day. Lily accepted my offer, merciful Heaven, but I have much work to do. I haven't sung in ..." He paused and hung his head for a moment. "Twenty-five years. I'm moving my camp to her back yard. If we go now, we can get back in time to get her to church." He shook out his sleeping bag, then dropped to his knees to roll it up.

Henry chugged as much coffee as he could while dressing and hurried to the outhouse. The temperature, he judged by the slightly hollow sound of the snow under his feet, was still just below freezing. He gulped a glass of water and hustled into coveralls, wool socks, Xtratufs, hat, and mitts. He put a spare hat and gloves in his pockets along with a handful of granola bars and a flashlight. He followed Squint out the door and paused with him on the porch to gather snowshoes.

"How is Albedo?"

"God smiles on little Albedo. He's up and around a little, drinking and eating. He will have scars, bless him."

Henry still had the imagery in his head of the shivering, bloody little dog being sewn up and was greatly relieved to hear he was doing well. He'd never heard of a dog being attacked by a coyote before. He remembered seeing the arrow in the coyote in Squint's drawing, but hesitated asking about it. He assumed it was symbolic. They approached Ms. Walton's house quietly and Squint set his huge sack on the porch. They went around to the back and put on their snowshoes. Not far behind the house was a flat spot under a massive spruce tree with hardly any snow. Squint stopped and spread his hands in a gesture of "what do you think." Henry nodded approval. They stepped over a narrow little creek not far beyond the new campsite and kept going.

## Nowhere Else To Go, but Dyea

In the predawn, the change from flat to steep ground was hard to see until they ran into it. Squint didn't break stride, stepping and stomping to make switchbacks and ledges in the snow up the hill. Henry followed with effort, stomping to firm up soft spots. They worked for what seemed an hour before both men took off hats and opened collars, in spite of the occasional bomb of snow falling from tree branches. Henry wished he'd brought a bottle of water and scooped snow to melt in his mouth.

When they got to a narrow bench with a screened view of the valley below, there was enough light to not only appreciate the elevation, but to see the top of a pole straining to hold a peak of camo print fabric. Squint studied the area around the pole for a moment, took off one snowshoe, put on gloves and began digging. Henry followed suit and carefully exhumed several ammo boxes, coils of rope, pet dishes, a rolled hammock and a folded beach umbrella. Squint, meanwhile, uncovered his tent, took it down and folded it. Henry put his snowshoe back on, asked where the latrine was and excused himself. He walked to a lower spot in the ledge to take a piss. He could see now how steep the hill was. He could see Ms. Walton's roof and his own house. Further up the valley he could make out the basic topography to figure where West Creek was and wonder that Squint came and went on a bicycle before the snow. He remembered the granola bars in his pocket and took out two, opening one and offering the other when he got back to where Squint still worked. The camp looked like an archaeological dig.

"Oh, thank you, brother." Steam rose from Squint's nearly bald head. "We'll tie the boxes to the rope and lower them down." He pointed to a pulley Henry hadn't noticed attached to a huge branch extending out over the drop-off. Still chewing his last bite, Squint took an end of rope and squirmed up to the branch, feeding it through the pulley. He backed down with the threaded rope end in his hand and began tying the ammo boxes at intervals along it.

"This will be much easier with help, oh yes. You go down and guide the first box, I'll lower." Henry put on his hat and gloves. He got a firm grip on the handle of the first box and headed down, guiding the string of boxes beside the trail.

He'd forgotten to put on his watch before leaving home, but Henry's stomach told him it was mid morning when they got all the boxes, tent and miscellaneous items down the hill. Squint brought the rope as the last load, coiling it as he descended. Henry rested while he waited. The snow continued to settle and he thought it was firmer and more condensed than when they went up. Something poked out of the snow near the pile of gear that looked like a branch, but was too straight. He scooped away snow with his snowshoe toe. It was the end of a green arrow with white fletches. He reached down to pick it up, but it didn't move. He dug deeper and hit something, dug more and saw rusty fur, then legs, tail and a head with smears of blood in the snow around it. It was the mostly frozen, completely dead coyote. Indeed, it had an arrow in its butt.

When Squint got to the bottom of the hill, Henry showed him the body. He shook his head, nodded and then shook again, but didn't comment. He began ferrying gear away from the hill and Henry fell in line.

All the gear fit neatly under the big tree. Squint identified two branches he could hang his hammock from. They went to Ms. Walton's to fetch the bag from her porch and were surprised to see her open the door and poke out her head. She had curlers in her hair.

"Daylight savings starts today, thanks to politicians who like to screw around with our day. We all have to leave for church in forty-five minutes." She tossed her car key to Henry and closed the door. He figured he could run home, clean up, put on his watch, wolf down some food and get back. But maybe he didn't have to go. She'd said "we all."

"Squint, can you drive?"

"Oh, well, whether or not I can is moot, brother. I haven't had a license in ... twenty-two years." Henry took off at a jog.

The drive into town was fairly musical with Ms. Walton singing a few phrases in Latin and Squint answering or harmonizing from the back seat. He snacked on something that could have been nuts from a small bag. A wonderful smell came from a covered platter of deviled eggs Ms. Walton had slid into the back. The good smell in the confines of the small car made Henry wonder that Squint smelled as good as he did. The only odor Henry had gotten from him was very woodsy, like tree sap. The snowplow had left the road smooth with sanded corners and high berms on either side. Several people along the way were chipping away at the berm with shovels to access driveways. All the shovelers waved as they drove by. Henry had been worried about driving on snow and ice after so many years in warm climates, but it all came back to him. He remembered driving his mother everywhere she needed to go when he was in high school. He took pride in four-wheel glides and generally doing what he could to make sure she kept a white-knuckle grip on the dashboard. What a jerk I was, he thought. He eased gently into a parking space on 5th Street with minutes to spare.

Ms. Walton turned to address both men. "We're doing a few hymns today, join in as you feel comfortable, and, Squint, if you'd like to play I'm sure it would be appreciated." She gathered her mittens, purse and wicker briefcase. "Dinner after the service. I made a double batch to cover your contributions." She climbed out.

"More kindness than I deserve," Squint said, also getting out. He fetched the egg platter and took Ms. Walton's elbow to escort her into the church. Henry watched them go. He wasn't really keen on attending a Presbyterian service. His reservations weren't theological, he liked Presbyterians, but the place was filling with people he didn't know and he was still uncomfortable with his social status in a new community. He may not be the only felon, but he was a new one and fair game for any negative feelings anyone may have regarding felons. He hadn't had quite enough time to eat before the trip to town and his stomach would be audible several pews away. Probably something you wouldn't want for your first time in a congregation. He started walking. It occurred to him while driving that he should stop by the police station and pick up a driving manual for Alaska. He wouldn't need to pass a test to transfer his own license, but Squint would need to start from scratch. And Henry had a feeling he would become the driver of preference for Ms. Walton. Listening to them sing together he felt they had or were developing a strong emotional bond.

Dave was at the police department doing paperwork in the front office. "Henry, how's it going? Enough snow for you? Hey, what size boots do you wear?"

"Hey, Dave. Um, a twelve, usually."

"Perfect. I made a steal of a trade for a new set of skis this morning, barely worn. You can have my old stuff. And you can help me with something. I've been hearing that someone is shooting arrows all over Dyea. They're high up on fence posts, stuff like that, too high to reach and retrieve, but one was tangled in a horse's tail and the horsewoman is pee-ohed." Henry told him he hadn't seen anything except the coyote and relayed the story.

"Well, holy cow. I'm glad Albedo is doing okay. Ms. Walton is full of surprises. Does she know you're not in church? You sure don't want to skip out on the feed afterward."

"Well, I wanted to come see if you have a driver's manual."

Dave reached under the counter. "Here you go. You don't need to test to transfer a valid license."

"I was thinking of Squint. He said he hasn't had one in over twenty years and he and Ms. Walton, well, I think he may be a more desirable driver than I am."

"I see." Dave smiled. "Know what his real name is?"

"What?"

"Ee-vo. Spelled Y-v-o. Last name is Shkip. That's what he used to get his library card and I can't see a person making up a name like that. I looked him up, no criminal history. No history at all, actually. He doesn't appear to have done anything electronic since it was invented. I look forward to his application for a license."

"Huh. He's making a big effort to step out of the woods a little, so maybe you'll see him. Thanks for the book." Henry left and wandered up State Street. As he approached the corner of 4th, he was looking left, across the street at the grocery store, wondering if it looked open, thinking he should go in and find something to eat, and he bumped into someone on the sidewalk.

"Hey, watch it . . ." Minerva renewed her grip on a wide, covered baking dish with a smaller covered plate on top of it and looked up. She handed both to Henry with a smile. "Mr. Stillwater! Good thing you came along, I was about to drop the whole damn thing. You're late, too? C'mon, let's go." She hooked her arm in his and set a brisk pace to the church. She guided him to the side door and downstairs to a room with long tables filled with chafing dishes, platters and bowls filled with food. She cleared a spot for her dishes and he set them down. She led him upstairs and into a huge, warm room with wood pews, stained glass lighting and singing.

Several people smiled and nodded as Henry and Minerva found a seat near the back and took off their coats. He could see Squint, head down, at the piano and the back of Ms. Walton's head in the pew nearest the piano. A few other people looked familiar. At the end of the hymn, Kevin went to the pulpit and began a story about being bogged down and lost, but finding your way through the snow. He seemed to be winding it up when he made eye contact with a bobbing, clearly squirming little head in the front row.

"Eulah Kathleen, are you hungry?" He leaned down, listening

to the little girl, and a wave of giggling spread through the crowd. "You are? Me, too. Let's go eat." He raised his eyes and voice. "Thank you all for coming today and may God bless you."

Henry tried to fade back and away from the press of people, but Minerva began introducing him to one person after another and he was caught up in a slo-mo stampede for the social room. Two ladies finished uncovering everything, placing serving spoons and forks where needed and stacking plates with napkins and silverware as a very orderly but noisy line formed. Trying hard to hear and remember names, Henry was swept along. He fielded questions as well as he could; how did he like Skagway, was he looking to buy a car, would he be getting in on the co-op Costco order, was he entered in the ski race yet, and was he doing the ten or twenty kilometer track, and are energy stocks ever going to go anywhere? He sat at a table next to Minerva with a plate piled with enchiladas, stuffed grape leaves, spring rolls, cole slaw, curried broccoli, deviled eggs, and one massive hockey puck of a biscuit. He had eaten nearly all of it when he heard Kevin, involved with his own heap of food, murmur to him from across the table that there was a break in the dessert traffic and that a person should get while the getting was good. Henry excused himself and went, coming back with a piece of pecan pie, a brownie and a mound of Ambrosia.

People were starting to say good-bye to each other when the one who'd asked about energy stocks slid into the chair next to Henry. "Those big ups and downs in the Dow Jones this winter scared the crap out of me. I don't know if I have the stomach for the stock market."

"I'm really not a good person to—" Henry took his plate and began to rise.

"But what if it doesn't settle down, would I have been better off in bonds?"

Feeling sorry for the guy, Henry wished he had some Zoloft on him to share. He sat back down. "The market is going to go up and down, that's how it works. If you don't need the money anytime soon, just forget about it. Ignore the business news. When you need it, there will most likely be more of it than when you invested. If you want more of a short-term thing, yeah, go with bonds. But they're not going to earn as much as stocks. Generally." The guy thanked him and left. Henry put his plate and silverware in a tub. He wished he'd had a pile of money invested when the market went to eighteen thousand. But he didn't. He began looking for Ms. Walton and Squint. Minerva caught up to him.

"This was nice, wasn't it?" She smiled. "Are you coming in to town on Wednesday?"

"As far as I know." He hoped he was since he had made a commitment to meet with Esme.

"Come by the shop. We'll have coffee."

Henry nodded and turned to go, but stopped and looked at her. "Yes, it was nice, thank you. Thank you for bringing me." They both smiled.

When Henry got to the Honda to warm it up for Ms. Walton, he did a double take. There was a pair of skis with poles bungeed to the roof. In the back he could see a pair of boots. He'd forgotten all about Dave saying he could have his old gear. They were cross-country skis, longer and narrower than the ones Henry had been fairly good with at several trendy downhill resorts. He ran a hand down one ski and looked at the bottom. Waxless. Ms. Walton and Squint put her deviled egg platter in back with the boots and chatted about the Easter program music all the way home. Henry had his hands full with driving. The temperature was right around freezing making the snow surface slippery. After he put the car in the garage, gave Squint the driver's manual and said good-bye, he walked home alone, carrying the ski gear. Buttercup was waiting on the porch for him, eager to get inside and keep her regular date with his rug. He leaned the skis against the house and went in with her. He turned on a burner to heat what was left of Squint's coffee before going out the back door to the outhouse. There was a green arrow stuck in the wood over the outhouse door.

An afternoon nap after a little reading would have been the logical order on Henry's agenda, but the coffee perked him up. He closed his book, made a quick note about the church experience in his journal and dressed for outdoors, trying on the new ski boots. Buttercup went out with him and watched him put on the skis. She followed as he wobbled across the yard and started down the driveway. They turned left, with an improving rhythm, for West Creek. Buttercup stepped on the ski tails a few hundred times then came around to lead. Henry was happy to let her set the pace. For a clearly elderly dog with a fair layer of fat, she was surprisingly energetic and moved at a trot. Before they got to the bridge, a skier came out of a driveway to the right. Henry recognized the hat and braids.

"Buttercup!" Ruby stopped and took off her mitts, replacing them with lighter gloves from her pockets. "Who've you got with you?"

Henry took off his hat and shoved it in a pocket. "Your neighbor, Henry. We met the other evening... right about here, I think."

"Oh, yeah we did. You were looking for Squint and I was looking for this one." Buttercup butted her head into Ruby's knee and the girl leaned down to give her an ear rub. "Did you find him?"

"Yes, I did. We met at Ms. Walton's. Buttercup was Albedo's hero." He briefed her on the coyote story and showed her the spots he medicated on Buttercup's foot and ear.

"Oh, you poor thing! But what a brave girl." Ruby straightened up. "She is very protective, especially of little things. Well, I'm off through there," she pointed across the road, "I'm making a trail that will wind around through your yard, if you don't mind, and loop back here. And if you see my little brother, tell him he's dead for taking my new arrows. I gave him my old bow and he's supposed to use the old arrows."

Henry made the connection. Ruby was the archer in the newspaper article. "Um, green ones?"

"Yeah, have you seen any?"

"There's one stuck in my outhouse and one in the dead coyote." He told her what Dave said about arrows all over Dyea and in the horse's tail.

"Ooh, Dad's going to kill him for shooting at live things. I know where you're talking about at the base of the hill. I'll get the one out of the coyote and swing by your outhouse." She threaded her hands through the loops on her poles. "Buttercup, do you want to go with me or with Henry?" Buttercup looked up at Ruby then at Henry. She lumbered around to stand next to Henry. "Okay, see you later."

Ruby crossed the road, sidestepped quickly up over the berm, and was gone.

Not far up the road and yet before the bridge, Henry saw a hand-lettered sign on top of a huge pile of snow where a small road ducked under the trees to the left. It said "moving sale." Henry asked Buttercup, "What do you think?" She turned left.

The moving sale was just getting set up. Henry met Earl and Pearl, retired teachers, who were moving to Hyder. They wanted a quieter place, they said. Henry had started to introduce himself and tell them where he lived, but they interrupted him and each other.

"You're at the Winterbourne cabin. You'll be needing–" he said, picking up a few things.

"And some of these," she said, "Ruby said you'd be at the barbecue, we looked for you, oh, let me get a bag–"

"How about this sled, then we can put all his–"

"Yes, and you'll need a bunch of these when you fire up the greenhouse."

"You know, I don't think that boy Widget should be left alone with turkeys, Mother."

"You're probably right, dear." She turned to Henry. "We gave him our turkey pen and house. He wants to start a 4-H project." She sighed. Henry dug out his wallet. "No, no, we can't take money for this, you need it and we can't take it with us."

Henry thanked Pearl and Earl and towed his new red plastic sled filled with boxes and bags out the driveway. He found he could pull on the rope with one hand and steady himself with both ski poles in the other. He had to move as far to the side as he could to let a car pass. Two more cars turned in the drive as he and Buttercup got to the main road, the people inside looking intently at his sled load. He turned right. When he got to the spot where Ruby had climbed over the berm, Buttercup stopped and sniffed, then climbed over and disappeared.

Not two minutes later, a pickup stopped next to Henry. There was a snowmachine in the back with camping gear, snowshoes, coolers, buckets and tools. A bearded man Henry didn't recognize rolled down the passenger side window.

"Damn, I was hoping to get that sled off Earl. You Hank?"

"Um, yeah, Henry."

"The highway is open and we're going to Log Cabin to start hacking through this crap to lay out the ski race. We can use all the help we can get if you can come up with Darwin tomorrow."

Henry looked at the bearded man, a woman sitting next to him and another bearded man at the wheel. "I don't know what I can do to help, I'm pretty new to all this."

"You're breathing and upright, that's good enough for us. What kind of beer do you like?" The man suddenly had a very intent look on his face, then let out a long and loud belch.

## Nowhere Else To Go, but Dyea

"I don't guess I'm very fussy."

"Perfect, see you tomorrow." They drove away and Henry heaved on his tow rope.

## Nita Nettleton

# 11

As an adolescent and young adult, Henry believed wealth was the gathering and cultivation of money. As he matured and developed his skills, he could smell it, track it down, tree it, and bend it to his will. He used it as a lure for the traditional accessories of wealth: youth, beauty and stimulation. But that wasn't really his end goal. He loved the planning, the growing and the gambling. He believed without a doubt it was his identity, the only thing he was truly good at. Sitting in his warm cabin in Dyea on a dark Sunday evening in early March, listening to a documentary on lake bottom core sampling from the Alaska Public Radio Network, sipping hot chocolate and munching snickerdoodles, he reconsidered what wealth is.

The sled load of gifts from Earl and Pearl was a bonanza. If there had been any hills on the way home, Henry would have had to take his sled apart and relay his ton of goods like the stampeders did toiling up the Chilkoot Trail. On the porch and all over the cabin floor, he spread out bags of potting soil, seedling flats, fertilizer, clothesline, eyebolts, nylon rope, a tube-style skylight kit, a bag of lime ("For your outhouse," Pearl had said.), a tool belt with tools, a bucket with more tools, tubes of caulk, a gallon jar full of screws, nuts and bolts, two *Whole Earth* catalogs from the Seventies, a small catalytic heater ("For your outhouse when it's cold," Earl said.), a canner filled with canning jars and about a dozen little cans of spices, seed-sprouter, stovetop toaster, oven roaster full of odd kitchen utensils and *Orth's Dictionary of Alaska Place Names*. Henry looked up Hyder, learning it's the most southeastern community in Alaska. And very small. His loot also included an Alaska recipe book, dish towel with a palm tree graphic on it, huge ball of twine, roll of metal mosquito mesh, and a fancy tin of homemade dog biscuits with the recipe included. Henry would have to think about where to put everything, but in the meantime he just admired it all. It looked like... wealth. The problem was that he knew little to nothing of what to do with it. The only reason he knew what the toaster and seed-sprouter were was because they were new and still had papers stuck to the bottom with diagrams and tips for successful toasting and sprouting.

A new nuance of wealth occurred to Henry. He used to know just about all there was to know in his world, and that was a major component of his wealth. Now he was in a new world with rich new resources, but no knowledge of how to exploit them. He needed to learn. And he was eager to do it. As he tried to explain that in his journal, he realized he had come a long way from crawling into a hole to die. As he fell asleep he was trying to determine the best place to put up the clothesline. He decided to look for guidance in the *Whole Earth* catalogs in the morning.

The morning did not go as he planned. He was up early, fortunately, so was dressed and fed when Darwin arrived shortly after eight. Henry heard him loading his truck with firewood and went out to help.

"Hey, Hank. After we deliver this we'll head out. You'll need your passport."

Henry remembered the bearded belcher he met yesterday and his plea for help with the ski race track. "Passport?"

"Yeah, Log Cabin's in Canada. And I got an extra sleeping bag for you."

"Uh..."

"It's a great spot. Usually good snow, this last dump will make a sweet race course. Needs a lot of work, though. And we have to start building the aid station."

Henry thought about Canada, as in the cold and frozen north, cross-country skiing which he was new to, beer drinking people half his age or younger camping in the snow and couldn't really see himself in the picture. "I don't know how much help I could be..."

Darwin chucked a final piece of wood onto the truck. "Look at it this way, Hank. A bunch of loose cannon yahoos with machinery and sharp tools need an organizer type. Torch knows the lay of the land, can find the markers and drives the snowmachine. It's better if he doesn't handle fire. Bucket is a good mechanic and can work like a demon all day long with supervision. Sleet can cook, stop bleeding and shovel snow faster and better than anyone around. They're the basic crew, then other people come to help as they can. It really all goes better when we have someone like you. You'll see when we get there. It'll be fun. School's out this week, so we could have extra help."

The firewood delivery was to Ruby's house. A tall woman with auburn hair in a bun and a sulking, foot-dragging medium size boy with his hands jammed into his pockets came out to greet the truck as it nosed into the yard and parked.

"Ms. Devine, Widge." Darwin got out and touched his hat brim. "You care which end of the wood shed?"

"Left side, Darwin, thanks. Chick likes to rotate. Who's your helper?"

Before Darwin could introduce him as Hank, Henry spoke up.

"Henry, Ms. Devine. I've met your daughter, Ruby, and Buttercup." He hadn't realized until this moment what bugged him about the name Hank. It's what Anne and Claire called him. His parents called him Hal. Most of his business contacts called him Ford since his cards read 'H. Ford Stillwater.' It was Anne's idea. He never really liked it.

"Oh, yes. Ruby told us. You should have come to the barbecue. She and her father left early this morning to fly to Ketchikan for an archery meet and a fly-tying clinic. Buttercup's lingering over breakfast. This one," she wrapped her fingers around the boy's neck, "is Widgeon. He planned to go along to Ketchikan, but screwed up big time and is here with me all week. Getting the seeds started and cleaning out the greenhouse."

The boy drooped further, seeming to hang from his mother's grip.

"Well, Widge, can you help us with this wood first?" Darwin began unloading and the boy leaped in to help. Ms. Devine went back to the house.

The three men set up a line with one in the truck tossing, one below catching and tossing to the third in the shed. Darwin asked Widge what happened.

"Oh, the damn old arrows Ruby gave me don't shoot straight and just bounce off things, so I borrowed her new ones. She wasn't going to tell Dad, but then the cops called. I got grounded."

"How long?"

The boy shrugged. "Dad said until I turn twenty-one. I'm only nine now, so that's twelve years. Or until I find all the arrows. Then Mom told me I would be a big help in the greenhouse, but I heard her tell her garden buddy on the phone that she was stuck all week with me underfoot. And they all wonder why kids run away."

Darwin hopped down from the tailgate. "You guys finish, I'll go settle up with Ms. Devine."

Henry signaled to Widge to climb up and toss and that he'd catch. "Are you named for the bird or the airplane?"

"The plane. Dad used to have one. He calls me Widget, but I don't really know what that means."

"It's like a gizmo. A thingamajig. Something useful." He got a skeptical look from the boy. "And what your mother said, don't take it too literally. There's what she says to you, what she says to other people and what she really feels. Totally different."

"I know. She and her gardening friends all say how super busy they are all the time and complain about it, but they really aren't. I say stuff like that all the time, too, I guess. If you look like you're not busy, someone always comes up with something for you to do, whether you want to do it or not."

"Right. Then you don't have time to do your own stuff." Like mess with your new loot from the neighbors, Henry thought. Mrs. Devine, Darwin and Buttercup came out of the house.

"So, Widge," Darwin began, "we need help getting ready for the ski race and your mother says you can go if you'll work hard and stay out of trouble. You want to go?"

The boy's eyes went wide and he grew about six inches. "Yeah!" Buttercup caught the excitement and began dancing, wagging and woo-wooing. "Can Buttercup go, too?"

Subtle facial signals passed between Mrs. Devine and Darwin. "She can take a nap when she gets tired," he said.

She said, "Go get your gear, Widge. I'll get paperwork for both of you to cross the border and pack some sandwiches." The boy ran for the house.

Darwin's truck labored up the Klondike Highway. The back was filled with brush cutters, rakes, machetes, a cooler full of food, camping mats, sleeping bags, blankets, skis, snowshoes, a bow and arrow set, and a huge yellow dog. The cab was full of serious man talk.

"I never meant to hit the damn horse," Widge explained. "I needed practice with a moving target."

"So you can learn to hunt goats or moose." Darwin waved as they passed the U.S. Customs station. "Good point. Still, your dad's right, you can't be shooting at live things for practice."

"I know the coyote was just a lucky shot. He was circling around the chicken coop and I aimed for his head, but he jumped over the fence. I can't believe I really hit him. I wish I could have seen him after Buttercup got through with him."

"It was pretty gory," Henry said. "Albedo and Buttercup were lucky he was already wounded. Could have been a different story."

"So why did Squint move down by Ms. Walton's? He had such a great spot with a view and he could pee over the side of the hill whenever he wanted."

"He wants to help her with the music for Easter and that takes a lot of practice, and you've gotta have the piano."

"Oh. Why didn't he just move into the tepee?"

"Huh... I don't know."

"Would have been dryer when all the snow melts."

"Yeah, dryer."

"And room for his bike out of the weather."

In brilliant sunshine over the pass at the Canadian border station, Henry kept his mouth shut and handed his passport across to Darwin. The border officer looked at the passports through huge sunglasses, asked if they had any guns, asked Widge if his mother got her seed order yet and rubbed Buttercup's ears. Widge offered that he wanted to grow heritage turkeys this year. The officer said they were delicious. It was just a few miles past the customs station to the highway pullout called Log Cabin. Darwin told Henry it was a camp on the gold rush trail and the tracks of the White Pass & Yukon Route railroad passed through it. A large parking area was plowed out and the tops of the outhouses were barely visible over a huge snow bank. They parked in a row of several vehicles next to the truck Henry saw the day before. Darwin got as close as he could so access to both trucks' gas tanks was too tight for a "thieving bastard with a siphon hose." They got out and stretched their legs, all four took a piss in the snow. They could hear the whine of a snowmachine in the distance.

Darwin took a folded map out of his shirt pocket and opened it flat on the hood of the pickup. "We're here. The race route starts over there and loops around here. The big aid station is here." The site was marked with a pencil drawing of a skull and crossbones. "Same place as last year."

"Is it a building?" Henry asked.

"Not exactly. It's whatever the theme is each year and built out of snow. And it's a big fat secret until it's done. I've got instructions here from the guy who comes up with the designs." He got another paper and unfolded it. "Pretty cryptic. We lay the foundation, whatever he wants to have done when he gets up here right before the race. We can't do it too early because it may get buried or melt too much." Darwin studied the drawing and frowned. "I don't know what the hell this will turn into, but he wants long bowed walls and a circular thing."

"All out of snow?"

"Yep. And as many extra blocks as we can make and some big snow balls."

"Let's go! I want to use the snowshoes. I can shoot better from them than my skis." Widge climbed onto the tailgate and began pulling things out the back of the truck. They stacked gear on Henry's new red sled, put on skis and snowshoes and loaded up backpacks with tools. Darwin handed Henry a pair of sunglasses from the glove box, told Widge to put his on, and led the way on a trail over the snow bank and across glittering, white snow. The snowmachine sound got louder as they approached the spot on the map where they were to build the aid station. Two sleds of gear were nearby and several people worked filling square buckets with snow, packing it down, then popping the formed blocks out in a row. Henry was reintroduced to Sleet and Bucket and joined them in block making. Darwin very seriously handed off the aid station plan to Henry, then he and Widge followed a snowmachine track to find Torch and a man named Mc D. Two other snow block makers, Hort and Karin, were introduced at a beer break.

"Henry, Yukon Gold or that piss water PBR your misguided countrymen brought?" Hort pushed up the sleeves of his sweater and dove into a huge cooler. Henry started to say it didn't matter, he wasn't particular. In fact, he hadn't had any beer in over two years. He'd had a celebratory scotch with Jason when he was officially signed out of prison, but didn't really enjoy it. Scotch wasn't the same. Maybe it never would be. He missed enjoying it, not the scotch itself. But beer, now that actually sounded good right about now. He'd been a Bud man as a teen and in college he tended toward micro brews. Still...

"Hort! Bring me a Molson's, eh? I've got your sandwich." Karin walked back from a smaller cooler with a red maple leaf graphic on the side, turned her bucket upside down and sat down on it. "Oh, don't you just love it out here? Sleet, that's a new jacket, eh? Did you get that through your pro deal?"

Sleet got up from the bucket she'd just sat on and mimed a modeling walk, showing off her jacket. "Yes, it's a Marmot, minimalist in every way except the price!" Both women laughed. Hort flopped down on the snow and handed Henry a Yukon Gold before opening his own.

"So," Hort took a long pull of his beer. "We should start building something. Who's got the plans?"

Henry got the paper out of his pocket and opened it on the snow in the middle of the seated group. "Okay, this is north, that way, right? So we want six-foot-high bowed-out walls here and here, about ten feet apart. Next to it, we want an upright cylinder about eight feet diameter as tall as we can make it. Doesn't look like they're quite touching."

"So what the hell is it?" Bucket leaned in and frowned.

"Hey, we'd have to kill you if you knew, eh?" Karin laughed and took a bite of her sandwich.

Hort snorted. "Looks like a missile storage and launch facility."

"No, but what is it really?" Bucket persisted.

Sleet stepped back and stretched. "The theme is Babes in the Woods. So it has something to do with that. And it has to be big enough to shelter the beverage station and first aid area. In case the weather goes south."

"The weather always goes south this time of year," Hort sighed. Everyone laughed. "But that's kind of a gruesome theme, don't you think?" Now everyone looked puzzled, so Hort went on. "It's an old children's story, from back when children's stories were scary, about two orphans abandoned in the forest and they starve to death and robins pile leaves on them."

"Gross," Sleet said. "You're kidding."

"I remember hearing that now," Bucket said, "at trivia night at the Red Onion. That's where the phrase came from, but Disney and everyone else got hold of the story and no one dies anymore, no robins bury anyone and it's just a metaphor for being small and vulnerable, implied innocent, in a big, implied corrupted, world." Everyone stared. "What?"

The sound of a snowmachine caught their attention. Torch drove into view with Buttercup on the seat between his knees and towing Darwin on Henry's skis. Mc D followed on a second machine with Widge sitting backwards behind him, bow up and arrow at the ready. They got sandwiches and drinks and joined the group.

Henry took a metal tape measure out of his pocket and began measuring and marking the locations of the walls. Widge ate his food in about five seconds and came to hold the end of the tape for him. They discussed markers for the locations and decided they needed sticks. Widge offered to cut some, Henry lent him his pocket knife.

By late afternoon, two long convex wall stems stood where they were supposed to and a round tower was begun next to it. The areas inside the walls were flat and packed. Hort and Karin said they had a dinner party to go to in Whitehorse, gathered their gear, said good-bye and headed for the parking lot. The others went back to work. Sleet, Henry, Bucket, and Widge formed and stacked blocks, Torch and Mc D drove off to work on the back trail with Darwin cutting brush. Buttercup sprawled on Henry's coat where he spread it on the snow for her. There was no wind and the air felt warm as long as he kept moving. Widge worked pretty well for about an hour carrying filled buckets for Bucket to place and dump. When he started to droop, Sleet suggested he roll up a big snowball to use for target practice. As soon as she said the words, she remembered another part of the plan.

"Oh! Snowballs!" Sleet called to Henry, "Where's the blueprint? We need to make snowballs." She looked at the paper he held. "These are just plain round balls, different sizes, a set here and here."

"For some kind of animal figures?"

"Who knows? All this is just a framework. The Master will pack snow on like plaster and cut out doors and windows. You won't recognize it when he's done."

"Yeah, last year I had no idea we were building a pirate ship."

There was still full daylight when the trail crew came in and turned off the machines. The builders welcomed the signal to lay down their shovels and stack their buckets.

"Kind of reminds me of something ancient," Mc D said. "Like

ruins. Tidier, though." Sleet heated a pot of chili over a camp stove and served it with cornbread and cut raw vegetables. Everyone sat on sleeping pads to eat. Henry opened the tin of dog biscuits he brought for Buttercup, but they looked pretty good so he passed them around after giving her a few. Kind of nutty, he and Widge agreed. McD asked to be excused as Mrs. Mc D in Carcross expected him home. He said he could come back in a couple of days, gathered his gear and drove out to the parking lot.

Darwin settled down with a Dr. Pepper and looked across the open area to two small tents in the trees on the south side. "I see Bucket, Sleet and Torch have a place to sleep, but we forgot to bring a tent, Widge. What are we gonna do?"

The boy looked at the tents and delivered a heartfelt, "Oh, man," in an ascending whine. After just a few seconds of thought he brightened, jumped to his feet and bellowed, "A fucking snow cave!"

Henry had finished his chili, corn bread and dog biscuits and didn't want to seize up from sitting very long, so got up to help Widge select a site and begin building their sleeping quarters. Neither wanted to make any more stinking snow blocks, so they did what Henry's Boy Scout troop did a million years earlier in the Adirondacks. They piled snow into a mound, packing it down as they piled with shovels and the occasional belly flop. When the mound was about the size of a VW bus, they began to tunnel into it from the base. They took turns removing snow from the inside and adding more snow to the outside. Widge suggested they could rent it out to people coming later in the week and charge even more during the race. Henry built up the door area, elongating it like a classic igloo entrance. Buttercup went in when they were finished to inspect it. When she came out, she circled the structure and peed on the east side of it.

Darwin unpacked sleeping bags from the sled and Widge

brushed his teeth while Henry carefully shaved snow from the igloo ceiling to raise and smooth the sleeping platform. When he finished, a tarp went in first, then pads and sleeping bags. Widge was the only one who brought a pillow. He said it was because he was the only one with a mother to think of stuff like that for him. Henry said he would use Buttercup, but Darwin said he'd have to arm wrestle him for her.

Torch wanted a campfire, but no one wanted to mess up the clean snow with fire remains. They hadn't had one the night before. Darwin excused himself, put on snowshoes and went to his truck. He came back with a chain over his shoulder dragging the chunk of metal, about four-foot square, that covered the rusted-out part of the bed of his truck. Everyone scattered to collect dead lower tree branches while there was still enough light. The fire was modest, but welcome and lasted a couple of hours. Henry drank another beer and explained the difference between bear and bull markets to Bucket. Sleet and Torch sang a few tunes from Grease. Everyone danced and howled.

The boys in the snow cave packed in like sardines, alternating head or foot first and Buttercup refused to be anyone's pillow. She made a spot for herself in the middle on a pile of coats, at Widge's feet. Henry was just about asleep when he heard Bucket call out to him.

"Hey, Henry! I just remembered. You found the Baby Jesus in Ms. Walton's garage, I hear. Not that I put it there or know anything about it, but I was planning to bring it out here. It would have been the quintessential Babe in the Woods, right?" The response in the camp was groans and laughter, then everyone said, "Goodnight, Bucket" in turn.

After a breakfast of instant oatmeal, fruit, nuts, coffee and/or beer, the whole crew worked on the aid station walls and snowballs.

## Nowhere Else To Go, but Dyea

The trail was as good as they could get for now.  By midday the bucket carriers were traveling a fair bit from the fresher snow the bucket fillers shoveled. They had used up all the loose snow around the mysterious structures. The snowballs were rolled from the edges of the clearing and measured for accuracy.

"I think that's as high as we can go on the tower without ladders," Sleet said at about two in the afternoon. "Doesn't look like anyone else is coming today.  And we're running out of food."

"We could make a circular stair out of snow blocks to keep going," Torch said. "But we'd still be out of food."

They packed up and cleaned up, raking out the snow around the work site.  Torch said he'd get with McD to finish the basic trail work and come tidy it up a few days before the race. The rest of the crew would report to The Master and get their next set of orders. While clearing U.S. Customs on the way home, they learned there had been another avalanche in the night and the road had just reopened.  That's why no one else came to help.   And they learned from one of the border agents that Ruby recovered all the arrows Widge had borrowed from her except one.  There was still one somewhere in Dyea and he would be in the doghouse until he found it.

Henry was really looking forward to warming up his house, getting into fleece pants and slippers and sacking out on the couch when he got home. After Darwin dropped him off and left, he clumped onto the porch and went in. He hadn't noticed the potting soil was gone from the porch, but surely did notice everything he'd left spread out on the floor was put away. And that the house was warm. There were flats filled with soil balanced along the back of the couch, on the kitchen counter in front of the window and on his bed where the bedroom window light fell strongest. The air in the house was moist and musty.

There was a note on the table. "Thanks for taking Widge, I'm sure he had a better time with you guys than he would have had with me. Squint, Ms. Walton and I got your greenhouse cleaned up and went ahead and started seeds for you. Here is the guide. You should make labels. Keep everything moist, but don't overwater. Lorelai Devine. PS– I didn't realize how blind Ms. Walton is. I'm making an appointment for her with the guy who comes from Juneau. You and Squint will have to figure out how to make her go. She has issues with doctors." There was a drawing at the bottom of the paper of all the flats and a list of what was planted in them. Vegetables, mostly, but also a few names Henry thought sounded like flowers.

# 12

Henry ate the last of his snickerdoodles with a cup of tea, listening to the quiet, before bed. His house was not at all the sanctuary cave he expected it to be. People came and went, making decisions about the house and immediate area, his immediate area, as they pleased. They did it without consulting him and without him even being around. It was like prison; he had no privacy whatsoever. The cookies and tea began to do their job and nudge him toward calm and content. He wondered if it was the invasion of his personal space or that other people made decisions that bothered him. He had called the shots for a long time, for himself and others. At that thought, he snorted and said aloud, "And that worked out real well, didn't it?" It's not like anyone took anything. In fact, they gave and very generously. He broke down particular instances and had to admit none of them alone really bothered him. Mostly they delighted him. Therefore, this was not a negative thing. Sure, he had no idea how each day would go until it went, but he was engaged, educated and . . . not even a little bit lonely. He tried to remember the last time he'd camped out, in any season. He hadn't since Boy Scouts. He thought no one would get any sleep in the snow cave, but Widge was out the minute his head hit the pillow and Darwin was right behind him. Henry barely had time to enjoy the sensation of settling down in an igloo and he'd fallen asleep, too. He looked around on the table for his journal to start a new list – things to do again – and put camping on it. He smiled and told himself he didn't need a list like that. "It'll come around again." He didn't feel like writing in his journal, anyway.

*Ellen Dieffenbacher had just finished her final exams and had a bus to catch. She was going home for a visit before graduation. She already had job offers and figured she may be too busy to get back for a while. The scarf her mother had sent her for Christmas had to be somewhere in Henry's dorm room. They'd already looked in all the drawers and behind the desk. He pulled out the bed and she lay across it to look behind. Just as she closed her fingers around the scarf and whipped her arm out with a whoop of victory, he dived down to roll her over. Her elbow smacked his forehead. They laughed and wrestled, she agreed to take a later bus before he got through the buttons of her shirt. They held each other and talked until she had to run for the last bus. He never saw her again.*

Henry woke up with an erection for the first time in over two years. But there was barely time to acknowledge it, let alone do anything about it. He heard quick footsteps on the porch and knocking at his door. He scrambled up and out and let Widge and Buttercup in. It was barely 7:30 and Widge announced he was on a mission. Henry had slept nearly ten hours and was slow to fully wake up. He wasn't really listening to the story of Ruby getting goosed by a Ketchikan boy and missing one of her damn targets completely. Henry made coffee and set out a Zoloft to take with breakfast. He'd forgotten to take it the last two days.

"The reason I came is because Mom told me to tell you she got an eye appointment for Ms. Walton and to put it on your calendar. She thought the doctor wasn't coming till next month, but it's this month and this week, even. It's today. At four. I said you wouldn't put something for today on your calendar, she said it's a figure of speech and to get going. I'm supposed to ask you if you think you can get the old bat there and let Mom know, because if not, then she has to call and reschedule." They looked at each other. "And I'm not allowed to go anywhere near Ms. Walton's house."

"Okay." Henry checked the flame under his percolator. "Watch this and when it starts to perk, don't let it do it too fast. I'll be back." Henry pulled on jeans, coat and boots over his long underwear and dashed out the door. It felt warmer than the day before and the squeak was gone from the snow underfoot. He heard the piano before he hopped up the steps to Ms. Walton's porch. He knocked.

Squint answered the door. "Good morning, brother. Come in." He stepped aside to let Henry in.

Not seeing Ms. Walton, but thinking she may be in the kitchen, Henry whispered the plan to Squint. He gave it a minute to sink in. "How do you think she'll take it?"

"Hard to say," Squint murmured. "She's a sensible woman, but I don't believe she's seen a medical professional in years."

"Yvo, is someone here?" Ms. Walton came from the kitchen carrying a tray with a coffee pot and two cups. She paused in the middle of the room.

"Yes, ma'am, it's me, Henry. Hal. I have a message for you from Mrs. Devine."

"Hal, you're early. Let me get another cup. Sit down." She handed the tray to Squint and went back to the kitchen. He set it down on a low table in front of a floral print sofa. Henry realized this could take awhile. He slipped his boots off and set them by the door, shrugged out of his coat and sat next to Squint on the sofa. He quickly raked fingers through his hair. Ms. Walton came back with a cup and sat on a chair across from the men.

"Would you please pour, Yvo? Go ahead, Hal."

## Nita Nettleton

Henry took a breath and began his pitch. "Mrs. Devine . . . would like to know if you are available at four o'clock today to meet with an eye specialist from Juneau. He's only here once in awhile and . . . it breaks her heart that you . . . someone who clearly appreciates the . . . the beauty of this world . . . are missing out on so much of it." Henry took the cup Squint handed him and sipped. Ms. Walton took her cup. Albedo, looking like a stitched-up little Frankendog, but with head and tail held high, trotted in from the kitchen and sniffed Henry's feet before curling up under the table. Ms. Walton held her cup in front of her chin, her face hard to read.

"That's very kind of Lorelei. I have been putting off getting my eyes checked." She blew gently over the surface of her coffee. "We planned to go to town at four since school is out this week, but we could go earlier if you're available to drive."

"Yes, ma'am, I am. Would 3:30 be all right with you?"

"That would be fine, Hal."

Henry gulped the rest of his coffee, rose, thanked his hosts and excused himself. He got home as Widge turned the flame under his percolator up and down, up and down, making the perking action race and slow, race and slow.

Henry chucked his boots and hurried to the stove. "What are you doing to my coffee?"

Small hands whipped down to the boy's sides. "Nothing. I think it's done."

Henry turned the flame low. "We cheated death, Widge. She went for it."

"Hot damn!" The boy wiggled a victory dance. "Dad and Ruby had a bet, Dad lost."

"Well, you can tell your mother we're a go at four. Do you think Ms. Walton has any insurance? A traveling eye doctor can't be cheap."

"The town'll prob'ly take up a collection. Wait'll they hear, this is huge!" He did one more dance wobble with arms over his head, then pulled a glove out of one jacket pocket and a book from the other. "Oh, can you take a look at this?" He set the book on the table. "Turkeys are different than chickens and there's some stuff I need to learn. Maybe you can help me. You comin' Buttercup?" The boy left, the huge yellow dog stayed.

Henry looked at the book. *Storey's Guide to Raising Turkeys* was three years overdue from the Juneau library. After breakfast and a bath, Henry made sure all his seeded flats were in the best light, learned that raising turkeys can be fun and rewarding and made an inspection tour of his greenhouse. The soil in the raised beds was churned and smoothed. Several large pots filled with soil were lined up underneath. The greenhouse was ready for the seedlings in the house, whenever they were ready for planting. He inhaled the musty scent and admitted to himself he was really looking forward to having a garden.

At 3:30, Henry had the Honda backed out of the garage and his backpack in the back. Squint and Ms. Walton carried grocery bags to toss in the back and got in. Ms. Walton seemed a little anxious, but Squint sang a tune and she joined in, relaxing. When they got to State Street at the north end of town, Squint murmured directions to the clinic. They got there a few minutes early.

"Hal, would you mind waiting here? I shouldn't be long." Ms. Walton fussed with her purse. "Then you can leave the car at the store and I won't need you until practice is over at eight."

"Surely, no trouble at all."

Squint went into the clinic with Ms. Walton. Henry watched them walk to the door. She appeared to lean slightly on his arm. His head was turned toward her the whole way. Henry felt a little pang of envy. He made a mental note to ask Squint if he preferred to be called Yvo now. He'd heard the basics of Squint's story but wondered how Ms. Walton got from a medical career and advanced music training somewhere to living alone in the woods at the end of a fjord, throwing rocks and singing in a church choir.

After about forty-five minutes they came out and got in the car. Ms. Walton sank into her seat and closed her eyes. Henry started the engine and headed south on State Street. They passed the library and he saw Esme's car at the curb.

Ms. Walton sighed and opened her eyes. "Well, what's done is done. Yvo, it was very kind of you to help me through that. I can't see for shit right now, so if you would, here is my list for the store." She handed back a slip of paper. Then she handed back her cowhide purse. "I think I'll just go to the church and practice until the others arrive." She closed her eyes again. Henry drove to the church and Squint helped her inside. He came back out and got in the front seat. Henry asked what happened at the clinic.

"Wonderful things," Squint said with a deep, gratified sigh. "She's dilated now, but that will pass. She has new glasses ordered, praise God. Medicare will cover most of it and the angel at the clinic is going to do her paperwork for her. Meanwhile, I paid cash for the doctor and the glasses. I'll be reimbursed, but even if not, I'm happy to help. She'll be able to see further than the end of her nose. We went berry-picking in August and she was lost as soon as we left her yard. Please thank Mrs. Devine for me. Oh, can you drop me at the police department? I still have time to do my driver's test."

"Hey, that's great, Squint. Oh, I've been meaning to ask, would you rather I call you Yvo?"

"Call me Squint or call me Yvo, but don't call me late for supper, brother." The formerly squinted eye matched the smile lines of the other eye. Henry laughed and made the requested stop at the police department. He parked the car at the grocery store and checked his watch. Minerva had asked him to stop by for coffee. He hustled over to Broadway and entered the bookstore.

## Nowhere Else To Go, but Dyea

"Mr. Stillwater, how nice to see you!" Minerva's gold tooth flashed and matched her gold hoop earrings. Her hair was pinned up in a chaotic pile on top of her head and a few corkscrew curls danced over her abalone ears. Henry realized he was staring and looked away. "Do you have time for coffee? I just made a fresh pot." She slid off her stool behind the counter and headed for the room in the back of the shop. "Come on back."

Henry followed her into a small workroom and took the chair she slid out before getting two mugs off a small shelf over a coffee maker. Bookshelves lined the upper walls and corkboard filled with notes lined the wall areas over the desk and worktable. She poured, turned, handed Henry a mug and sat with the other on the only other chair. He mumbled a thank you and took in the wonderful smell from his mug before taking a drink. It was rich and nutty.

As if reading his mind, Minerva giggled and said, "Rich and nutty, just like me." At his startled expression, she went on. "Don't worry, everyone calls this blend rich and nutty. And I'm not all that rich."

They looked at each other over the mug rims. "I Googled you."

Henry set his mug on the table. "And?"

"You didn't fight your conviction very hard. Bad lawyer?"

"Good lawyer. Any fight at all was her doing. I wanted to take my lumps. I'll probably never stop feeling I need to atone. Maybe it's that way for everyone who really understands the extent of his or her law-breaking."

"As I understand it, the laws you broke were the kinds of things that change all the time, like policy and underwear. Pretty far from ten commandments kind of stuff."

Henry shrugged. "I knew it was illegal, I did it anyway. I re-hashed it daily for about a year after the settlement, but now I don't think about it very much. Where did you read about it?"

"Newspapers. Dallas, mostly. You can get just about anything online now."

Henry studied Minerva as she spoke. One little curl kept bobbing in front of her right ear. "Should I Google you? How did a clearly well-educated woman from, I'm guessing by your accent, Vermont, come to this little western outpost?" He paused with one arched eyebrow then checked his watch. "I'm headed to the library to meet Esme. I'm helping her with her geometry. I could log on after that and dig up your story."

"Well, it wouldn't be very interesting reading. Besides, I'll tell you everything. Why don't you come to my house after your tutoring session. Have supper with me."

"Don't go to any trouble. I don't know how long we'll be. Then I need to hit the grocery store and take Ms. Walton home after choir practice. And…" He stopped and dropped his eyes, taking a sip of coffee.

"You should have time between the library and church. I live right across the alley, north side of the church. Green door. You can't miss it. You were going to add, 'and why am I so interested in you.'" Her eyes bore into him.

He squirmed a little. "Yes."

She let one side of her mouth lift in a smile. "You speak well and don't talk much about yourself. You don't feel anyone owes you anything. You're kind to your neighbors. I hear Buttercup likes you. Do you play poker?"

He set his cup down and stood up. "Yes, I do."

"Perfect," she said. "I hope to see you later."

At the library, Esme had two geometry chapters' worksheets done and just needed to go over them with Henry. After that, she wanted to read her speech to him. For her entry in the Oratory Contest she wrote about home. In the second paragraph, she started to cry. "How am I going to do this in front of a room full of people if I cry every time?" She wiped her eyes with her sleeve.

"Well, it shows you care, certainly. That's a good thing. But you have to be able to keep going. Will your mother or Darwin be there? Sometimes it helps to pin your attention on one person who already knows how you feel about something. Make eye contact with everyone initially, but when you get to the emotional part, you just speak to that person."

"Mom will be there, but she'll be crying right along with me, so that won't help. Darwin might work. I'll read it to him and see what happens. How about you, will you be there? It's at the Eagles on the twenty-ninth."

"I guess I could be. Would it help?"

"Yes, it would. I know Darwin would feel better with you there. He's practicing his poem and figured out what he wants to talk about. He really liked your idea of talking to people on the way in, then personalizing what he says after the poem part. I think you'll be proud of him."

"I already am. I'm proud of you both. I'll be honored to be there."

With just a few things on his list, Henry made quick work of the grocery store. He recognized more people this visit and even made a little small talk with a few. He remembered the post office after he put his groceries in the car and jogged up to check the mail. Ms. Walton had a small stack including one of the pre-paid postal mailers. He peeked at the name on the mailer. It was for Mr. Yvo Shkip. There was one letter size manila envelope and he noticed the addressee was himself. It was from the tax accountant A. J. hired to prepare his tax return. She had told him he was on his own after this one. He jammed it into the front pocket of his pack. He put the other mail in a grocery tote and into his main backpack bag. He hurried south through nearly deserted streets and made one last stop before moving the car and getting to the alley behind the church.

Henry got to Minerva's green door by 6:45. When she opened the door, she was backlit with warm, yellow light and surrounded by a savory vinegar smell.

"Henry, come in. You're just in time for some cabbage rolls I put together this morning. I needed bread, but got that on the way home. Did you see the Greek yogurt at the store? That usually goes pretty fast. Ooh, what's this?"

Henry handed her a bottle of wine before leaving his boots, jacket and pack at the door. "I took a chance you like dry reds, but should have gotten something European."

"Argentine Malbec, well you can't go wrong with that. I love it. Will you join me?" She fetched two glasses from her tiny kitchen and directed Henry to an overstuffed chair in her small living room. She opened the bottle and brought it to a small table. While she poured he looked around the room. There were bookshelves all the way around, floor to ceiling, with more books on the deep windowsills. There was no dining room, just a wide counter with stools off the kitchen. He could see a stair out the back of the room in a dark hallway "Bath downstairs, two bedrooms and another bath up. But the small bedroom is my office. Not really set up for entertaining or guests. I have an intern in the summer for the newspaper, but she stays above the bookstore in the paper office. Like in the old days, sleeping under the type table. Except now we have a computer desk for her to sleep under."

Henry sipped his wine. It was heady and felt good in his mouth and on down to his stomach. He couldn't remember the last time he drank wine. "You said you do the paper by yourself in the winter. Isn't that a lot of work with the bookstore?"

"I have Ruby part-time in the store and really, most of the news comes to me. I don't have to chase it down. I take a few pictures. I put it all together on the computer, people who want to advertise come to me, too. But there is a story you can help me with. I am very curious, as I'm sure my readers are, in a Mr. Yvo Shkip, aka Squint." She sat on the edge of an armchair across from Henry. "He lived in the woods for years, barely spoke, ducked in and out of the post office and occasionally the grocery and hardware. Then suddenly he's cleaned up and playing the piano and singing in the Presbyterian Church. I always assumed he was on the run from the law. Maybe not."

"He's an interesting character," Henry said. "He told me about his past when I met him, so it doesn't appear to be any big secret. I can tell you he's quite an artist. And he's been studying fungus in terms of climate change. I think he would be willing to speak with you. He took a driving test today. I may be losing my job as Ms. Walton's driver. Plus, she got her eyes examined and ordered new glasses today and could be driving her own self again soon."

"Really? Holy shit. Aren't you a catalyst for changes in the 'hood!"

"It's nothing to do with me, I'm just a messenger and laborer."

"You're too modest. I ran into Mrs. Devine and Darwin, they both spoke highly of your help. And I hear Widge is counting on you to help him with his 4-H turkeys."

"That one sneaked up on me more than anything. The kid gave me an overdue library book on raising turkeys. I have no idea where to go from there."

"Well, I also heard that Earl and Pearl gave him a bunch of pen material that he's going to put up at your house. You and he are going to be partners. I just hope there's a Thanksgiving dinner in it for me." They both laughed. "You're sinking into that chair pretty fast, Stillwater. I'd better get some dinner into you." She got up and went to the kitchen.

After dinner Henry met his neighbors and started driving home. No one said anything for the first few miles so Henry replayed his visit with Minerva. In the agreeable light of her house and with wine and casual conversation on a variety of subjects, he looked at her more closely than he had in their previous encounters. She looked like... Cher. Yeah, that was it. Large dark eyes, elegant face bones, tons of hair. Not as tall. And her voice was rich and low. She planned to come out to Dyea on Saturday, when Ruby worked the bookstore all day, and ski. She hadn't skied in about a million years, she said, and was entered in the race. Her costume was a bigger concern to her than her skiing, but thought at least one practice session was wise. He smiled remembering her talking about it and making him promise to go with her.

When they rounded Dyea Point and headed for the mouth of the Taiya River, Henry asked how everyone else's afternoon went. Ms. Walton said the choir was sounding very confident and that Easter would be beautiful. Squint shared that he passed his written test and Hilda let him use her car for the driving part to just get it the hell done with, and he got an Alaska driver's license. Fortunately, he had thought to take his birth certificate since his library card was not considered sufficient identification. Henry mentioned that he got the mail, hoping Squint would look through it.

Squint got out the mail then turned on the dome light to read a short letter. "Oh, Lord," he said, shaking his head. "Sister Mary Reginald has been busted. Mother Superior says I shall not be doing business with her in our old arrangement, although the end result was for the greater good. There goes my income."

"Oh, for Pete's sake, Yvo," Ms. Walton said. "You are such a talented artist, people will pay you a lot more than a collection plate pilfering nun did. I think Lorelai belongs to a co-op with her pottery. She'll help you get started."

"Well," he said. "I suppose I could try something new. I believe I had run my course with angels. And Sister Mary Reginald never let me put fungus in the pictures." He and Ms. Walton began a fugue-style duet from "All the Bright Seraphim". Henry felt sure the snow banks and brooding overhanging branches in the headlight beams were singing along.

## Nita Nettleton

# 13

Buttercup was clocked in and ready to inspect the coop and pen when Henry woke up at five. He was pleased that he didn't need an alarm clock. Sunrise, according to his new Northern Light calendar, occurred at 3:43 on June 15. Father's Day, the calendar also advised. This bit of information shifted to the back of his mind for later. He bathed and dressed then met Buttercup for the inspection tour and the "Releasing of the Turkeys." She loved it when the heritage turkeys, three Narragansets and three Bourbon Reds, dashed out of the coop, through the pen and into the yard. She barked once to make sure they noticed she was on duty. Pecking and scratching commenced with little fuss after that. Henry liked the look of Widge's turkeys. The poults didn't look very promising when they arrived in April, but quickly put on weight, grew impressive feathers and got a routine established. Later in the morning, Widge would come to look for eggs, make sure there was water and to clean the coop. The manure pile, a gold mine according to the boy, was growing. He put a notice up at the post office that it was available by the bucket for a reasonable price. So far, several people had taken advantage of the excellent deal, however no cash had changed hands to Henry's knowledge. Widge reported receiving a skateboard, a set of leather-working tools, an old bomber jacket with cool patches, and a punch card for ten ice cream cones. Darwin suggested he not try to sell the raw product since there were other producers and the market was flooded, but collect seaweed and sawdust and make a special garden blend for a lot more money. Widge said he'd consult with his mother's master gardener group next time they met at his house.

In the greenhouse, Henry thinned his carrots and radishes. He had enough lettuce to start harvesting and the spinach was just about ready, too. The smell in the greenhouse was still earthy, but now with a vegetably top note. The potted flowers were getting crowded. It was time to put them out somewhere, but he didn't trust the turkeys to leave them alone. Maybe he should get some wire baskets and hang them along the porch. He watered everything and opened the greenhouse vents. Clear sky and dry air promised another scorcher. After breakfast he bagged the doggie biscuits he baked the evening before. The tin he got from Earl and Pearl was such a hit, he'd been experimenting with recipes. This batch had a salmon base and was a lot smellier than the pumpkin ones. He decided he'd better double bag them. There was an odd number left after bagging, so Buttercup got an extra one. She made it clear she liked the salmon better than the pumpkin. Henry told her he thought a little went a long way.

After breakfast Henry put clean underwear and a shirt in his backpack. The new calendar was to keep his work schedule on and showed he had two days back-to-back in town, so he would stay over. He wrote a note for Widge to be sure to lock the turkeys up before bed and to come early enough tomorrow to let them out. And to give Buttercup a bag of the new biscuits for breakfast. He tiptoed into the tepee just in case Squint was there and could possibly have slept through the turkey release. Since he installed the tube skylight and turned the tepee into a studio, he sometimes worked late and slept there. He'd essentially moved in with Ms. Walton after she got her new glasses and he got her to start taking his herbal mood adjuster, but confided in Henry that he missed sleeping outdoors. He hosted a painting basics class on Saturdays and several people came to work with him at other times. Lorelai suggested he send his fungus drawings to a nature magazine she subscribed to and helped him order supplies for printmaking. Squint often sang or whistled when he was working alone and Henry enjoyed listening. It was a pure, happy sound.

But there was no one in the tepee this morning. Henry took the bicycle they agreed to share and rode out to the main road. The roadsides were aglow with dandelions and a riot of greenery surrounding them. Sooty grouse hooted in the hills, varied thrush tweeted in the trees. Henry stopped at the Taiya River bridge to watch a black sow with a cinnamon cub stroll up the Chilkoot Trail. She'd scared the bejeesus out of him the first time he ran into her on the narrow road. She had basically ignored him then as she'd done at every meeting since, and he was getting used to her. After she was away from the main road, he rode on. There was hardly any traffic early on a Sunday. He stopped at a high vantage to look at the river and tideflat below. There were mergansers, gulls and a few great blue herons.

The ride to town was a real slog when Henry started doing it in April, but now he only breathed heavily on the uphill parts and never had to get off and walk anymore. He considered entering the marathon held the day before, thinking he might be able to do the half distance without dropping dead. But he decided to work at home instead. The chores tended to pile up if he didn't keep after them. Plus, Darwin had been bringing wood to store in the shed and he liked to keep it split and stacked in a timely manner. Squint helped with that. Darwin called them his geezer splitters and bragged they were faster than the machine. Henry doubted that, but liked that they were a lot quieter. Darwin was spending more time in Dyea since the new teacher who moved into Earl and Pearl's place needed a few things done around the house. Henry had assumed Darwin and Esme were a solid pair but had never really seen them together until the evening of the Oratory Competition. The way they looked at each other, made eye contact through their speeches and hugged afterward made it clear they were more like siblings. And Darwin seemed to find Calliope, the new teacher, pretty dang fascinating. According to rumor, he was learning to write poetry.

Henry was thinking about Darwin finding something un-mechanical or noncommercial that he was good at and nearly missed his turn for the shortcut to town. He remembered a part of Darwin's speech where he said his father made up little poems all the time and that's how he got Darwin to remember the way things worked or went together. And that Darwin had said earlier his dad was not a very good father. And here it was, Father's Day. The hill down past the old shooting range to the trail that led to the footbridge took a little more concentration, and Henry forgot where his mind was headed on the subject of Father's Day.

With the bike locked in a rack in the alley, Henry unlocked the bookstore. Sunday there was only one cruise ship in town so business would be slow. It was a good day for cleaning, straightening and putting out new stock. He found a list from Ruby of what she wanted where. He got the cash bag and set up the register then straightened the items on the counter and got a broom to sweep the doorstep and boardwalk. Several other people starting their workday called and waved to him from across the street and up and down the block. He picked up used drink cups, napkins and a few beer cans from the gutter and put them in the city trash can on the corner. The sun washed the streetscape, highlighting the bright colors of the buildings, and lighting up the dark green slopes and brilliant white snow remnants on the crags of the peaks surrounding the little valley. Henry thought Skagway looked its best in the morning.

A Juneau newspaper Henry hadn't looked through yet was next on his agenda when a young woman in a Park Service uniform came in the open door of the shop carrying a coffee cup and a wide, flat bag.

"Henry, I hoped you'd be here today. Not that Ruby wouldn't do it too, but you're easier to talk to. Here's a latte. I think you like hazelnut? I have to watch the time, I'm on the front desk this morning. My mom is coming next week and I found this in the co-op." She lay the bag on the counter and slid out one of Squint's new spring flower block prints. "She'll love this. But he didn't sign it. And he never comes to town anymore. Can you take it and ask him to sign it?" Henry started to respond in the affirmative when she went on. "Is he signing his stuff as Squint or Yvo? Squint seems a lot cooler. And do you think he'd put 'for Eleanor' on it, too? I've gotta run. Thank you so much!" And she was gone. Henry wrote a note and put it in the bag with the print. Then he enjoyed his latte.

Straightening up the postcard rack and note cards, Henry noticed a particularly nice blank card with a watercolor view of the Dyea valley on it. He bought it and put it in his pack. Getting his nerve up to write a letter to A. J. was taking time, but he wanted her to know how beautiful it was here and what his new life was like. He wanted to offer some kind of a relationship with her, but he wasn't sure if an explanation or apology were in order. He had no idea if she was even slightly interested in his life or whatever peace he might offer. He thought the sheer contrast of his old and new lives might interest her.

Late morning a couple from the ship came into the store. She was small, blonde, dressed in white tunic and capris with black accessories and pastel makeup. Her huge, shiny black purse caught Henry's attention. It was big enough to hide a small pony. He had been warned by Ruby to watch the bags. People take things, she said. No matter how well they're dressed, it's a recreational thing with some people. So he watched bags.

The woman smiled on her way in the door and lifted up zebra stripe sunglasses. "Oh! Books, honey!" She started a slow circuit around the shop. Her honey followed with no apparent enthusiasm for books and veered left when he saw the stack of newspapers on the counter. Henry kept his focus on the black bag.

"These are yesterday's," the man said, clearly disappointed. Henry started his memorized description of how and where the newspapers come from and that later in the day there may be something fresher. "But," the man said again, "you're selling yesterday's news." This is why Minerva and Ruby were so happy when Henry agreed to work a couple days a week at the shop. He had worked years and years with people. People who struggled to grasp what Henry was either talking them into or out of. Most people take a little time or cajoling to embrace a new concept. The man standing in front of the sales counter was trying to grasp the concept of day-old news. Henry was crafting a donut analogy in his mind when he pried his eyes off the huge black bag and looked at the man. He looked familiar.

Henry had always been good at remembering faces, but wasn't coming up with a name for this one. He hoped it wasn't from prison. Or from a courtroom. Or, for that matter, from anything having to do with the last year or so of Henry's business career. The man stood tall, had a trendy haircut, polo shirt, tan slacks. His skin was pale and he was pudgy around the middle, suggesting too much time at a desk. He looked at Henry like he was trying to dredge up a name, too. Before either man could speak, the man's cell phone rang and he fished it out of his pocket and answered it without moving away.

"G. Buckmeister Hill," he said into the phone. How could anyone forget a name like that, Henry asked himself. He remembered now. A few years ago Mr. Hill was putting together an investment in undeveloped gold properties in Mexico. Gold was booming, but Henry was not interested in the project. Buck, as he liked to be called, or the Buckmeister, hounded him for a period of weeks, offered dinners, cigars, even trips to go look at potential mines. But nothing on Mr. Hill's face indicated he connected H. Ford Stillwater, possible investor, with this clerk in the bookstore in Skagway, Alaska, selling old news. He set a lunch date with someone for later in the month and put the phone away, still standing his ground. "Ford," he said. "What the hell are YOU doing here? You know, not a day goes by I don't wish I'd listened to you and bagged the Mexican mine project. I broke even, but..." He shrugged. "What the hell ARE you doing here?"

"Buck," Henry said and extended his hand. They shook. "I made a few changes, downsized. I live here now." He didn't feel like elaborating.

"Well downsizing is all the rage now. I got into some blocks of ridiculously tiny houses with communal courtyards, selling like tiny hotcakes."

"You're on the Moonlight Sonata, right? I hear that's a very classy ship. How do you like it?" Old trick Henry used to use, keep them talking about themselves, but in a different context.

"It's great, about four grand a pop, but she's always wanted to take this cruise and it goes all the way to Seward, then we go to Denali, so it's the best trip with five star chefs, shows every night. I know a guy on the board of directors, so we got a suite you wouldn't believe." Buck looked at his watch. "We're just looking around before our helicopter tour, dogsledding or something."

Henry smiled and nodded. "Wow, today that'll be really spectac—"

"You know, Ford, I got something you might be interested in." Buck reached into his pocket and got a business card. "Give me a call." Henry took it and nodded again. Mrs. Hill or her substitute had finished her loop through the shop and left, Buck followed her out. "Good to see you, Ford, call me." They headed up the boardwalk.

Henry read the card and started, automatically, to slide it in his pocket. Before he could get it there, his hand detoured and dropped it in the trash. The last thing he wanted was some deal with G. Buckmeister Hill. Even if he had anything to invest.

Minerva came in at about one in the afternoon. She was flushed and wearing hiking clothes. "Henry, how's it going today?"

"Normal Sunday," he said, giving her a quick kiss on the forehead. "You're all sweaty, where'd you go?"

"Upper Lake," she said. "And women glow. Horses sweat, men perspire." She took a bandana from her shorts pocket and blotted her face. "You've got to get up there, it's so beautiful. I'd go again later this week if you want to."

"Okay. I got most of Ruby's new books shelved and did some cleaning. I brought you lettuce and a little spinach, it's in the fridge upstairs."

"Nice! I'm making lasagna for our dinner, this will be perfect. I need to go see your garden. And see how big the turkeys are getting. Do you think Widge is going to be able to whack them?"

"He's planning to sell tickets for a turkey shoot. Is the game on tonight?"

"Yep, at six. It's Cash's turn to host so there will be good music and refreshments. This ship leaves at five, you can close a little early. I'm headed home to jump in the shower. Do you want me to spell you for a break before I go?"

"No, someone brought me a sandwich to trade for a bag of the new dog biscuits. I'm good."

"Ooh, you are so self sufficient," she purred with a sidelong look, "I will see YOU later." Henry smiled and winked. Her glowing, alpine meadow smell lingered after she was gone.

At about 4:30, Henry had the register rung out and was about to lock up. He tossed something in the wastebasket and saw the business card he dropped in earlier. He got it back out, read it again, and slipped it into his shirt pocket. Maybe he should call the guy, see what he was talking about. What would it hurt? He turned the closed sign and went out, locking the door behind him. He turned to head for the alley and nearly bumped into the Buckmeister.

"Ford! Glad I caught you. I gotta run, but I wanted to just run this one by you, get you started thinking about it." He took a deep breath and launched into his sales pitch. He had a solid group of investors and wanted Henry to be a full-time consultant. "We need someone not in the pool who knows the business and can do the research. Salary or commission, your call. Easy money either way. And you could work from here." He looked up and down the street. "You got Internet, right?"

"Buck, I just spent a couple years in prison for similar work."

"Yeah, yeah, we just talked about that on the phone. Gives you perspective."

"It's a really nice offer. Let me think about it."

Buck started walking backward toward his ship. "Call me!" He turned and walked faster.

Over dinner, Henry told Minerva about running into G. Buckmeister Hill and the job offer. "People dream about offers like this. Getting to live wherever you want, working your own schedule."

"With other people's money," she said. "Sounds ideal. Best of all worlds. And easy money, as he said. So what's the problem?"

"I admit there are things I miss about having a lot of money. I miss the game, too. Watching the markets, working with the players." He fiddled with the hair down the back of his neck that caught in his collar. "I miss good haircuts. Exotic seafood."

"Oh, that reminds me," she said. "Chick wants you to go fishing with him this week, halibut. He was so impressed with the luck you brought to the boat for kings, he wants to try you out on flatfish. He can't take Widge yet and if he hooks a big fish he'll need help anyway."

"Poor Widge. Isn't there a statute of limitations on losing one of your sister's arrows? If he hasn't found it yet, what are the chances?"

"He took the arrow without permission, so there is no statute of limitations. It's like murder. You're a father, you should know the rules. It seems harsh, but we all know that kid is going to be a senator, at least, and the green arrow story will probably get him into office."

"Yeah, no doubt." Henry started clearing the table. "Today's Father's Day, you know."

"Did you get a card?"

"No. She's never sent me one. But I've been thinking about her a lot. I'd sure like her to come here and visit. Meet you all. Sit in on the game. One of her staff says she's a hell of a poker player."

The game started promptly at six. Cash had the table and folding chairs ready, trays of snacks on boards over sawhorses and Jimmy Buffet on the garage stereo. His wife didn't allow card playing and the suspected adjunct cigar smoking in the house. A cooler under the snack spread held ice and beer. Bucket won the dice roll to deal first and shuffled the cards several times before dealing.

"Ante up, gentlemen." Bucket had a small, aromatic cigar in his teeth. "The game is five-card draw." Henry, Chick, Cash, and Dave took their cards and studied them. Each took two chips from an equal pile in front of them and tossed them to the middle of the table. Just about every week there was a discussion about using real money, but Dave had to remind everyone each time that he couldn't play with real money. No one really minded. Cash had a huge set of chips so they could bet big and grow substantial pots.

The bigger problem was when Dave got a call to go do police work in the middle of a game. Before the arrow incident, Widge was attending with his father and learning to play. Everyone hoped the boy would find the damn arrow and come back. He added enthusiasm.

Chick, to Bucket's left, opened and the game was on. "Henry, you free to go fishing Thursday or Friday?"

"Yeah, Minerva said. I'd love to. Thursday would be better, I've got yoga Friday morning."

"How's that going?" Bucket took two cards. "The new teacher's name is Calliope? What the hell kind of name is that? And who can do yoga so early in the morning?"

"Like you'd know anything about that time of the day," Dave said. "I fold. I hear Darwin can do yoga that early in the morning." Everyone snickered. "And I hear there's poetry after the yoga. You in on that, Henry?"

"No, I have turkey and garden chores I like to get done early, so I go home after the yoga. I never would have believed, but it really is energizing."

"I'm sure that's what Darwin's after," Cash said. Everyone snickered again. "Where's Minerva?"

"Said she had some work to do," Henry said. "Chick, I've been watching the meter on the solar panels, I think you got the angle just about right. Plenty of juice."

"And all you run is the fan in the greenhouse. You could have appliances, you know. There's plenty of power."

"Like what?"

"Like a fridge," Bucket said. "Keep your beer cold."

Henry played three jacks and won the pot. "I could use a fridge for my produce and for the dog biscuits."

"I can't believe you're baking doggy treats," Bucket said, shaking his head. "How'd the salmon ones come out?"

Henry got a bag from his backpack. "Here, try one. Buttercup likes these the best so far, but I think they're too strong."

Bucket bit into one and passed the bag around. "Mmm, no, this is good. You're finally onto something. I'll take whatever Buttercup doesn't want. I'll use them on guide trips. Can't feed 'em to the guests unless we make them in a commercial kitchen and go through all the BS, but this is definitely guide fuel."

"I'll take just one card, please," Dave said with a wicked smile a few hands later and got everyone's attention. "I've been meaning to ask you, Bucket, about the Nativity scene on the back loop of the ski race."

Bucket snorted and took three cards. "Like I'd know anything about it, Dave."

"Torch told someone the whole story in the hardware store the other day and didn't realize I was within earshot. He feels terrible. Imagine my surprise as I came wheezing around the curve in the race to see a huddle of snowmen in a rude twig shelter with the Baby Jesus in his little manger in the middle. I thought I'd had the big one and died. The same Baby Jesus missing for so many years and miraculously reappeared in Ms. Walton's garage and then restored to the church. A very safe place in the church, I was given to understand. Spirited out just before the race, then just as sneaky, put back right after. How do you do it, man?"

"I think you're bluffing, Dave," Cash said. "I raise you five bazillion." He chucked five of the fancy purple chips into the pile on the table.

Bucket relit his cigar. "It was a preview of the miracle of Easter, you know? The original Babe in the Woods, risen from his tomb under the cupboard where they keep the hymnals just so I'm not the only one knows where they keep him in case he goes missing again, risen to bring his message of joy and whatever Easter is all about to the wretched racers in the ski classic. Damn, I fold."

"Well, I have to say, the effect was good. I stopped and took a picture." Dave raked in the pot. "And the aid station was particularly inspired this year. Huge bear cubs and bunnies in the end of a hollow log and a stump with a nest full of baby birds on top." The group raised their glasses and saluted The Master.

The last game of the evening was the Barter Round. Since they didn't use real money, the players agreed to a white elephant kind of thing. Everyone wrote the name or description of an item on a piece of paper, folded it up and bet it. The winner got all the loot. Since everyone wanted to keep his or her place at the table, the items were things the others would want. Henry wrote "potted petunia" on his slip. He had four pots growing like mad and just about to start blooming. Everyone paid close attention to each other's cards and tells, took their time and played to win.

## Nita Nettleton

# 14

Back home Monday evening, Henry was happy he didn't lose one of his petunias. He wanted to give the pink one to Minerva. She had a hook on her porch that would be perfect to hang it from. She loved pink and he imagined her face smiling up into a cascade of pink flowers. He was expecting pink, blue, purple, and mixed flowers from the four pots. He found three eyebolts in the jar of nuts and bolts he'd gotten from Earl and Pearl and screwed them into his own porch eave, next to the wire that Chick ran from the solar panels on the porch roof to the greenhouse.

Seeing the wire reminded Henry what Chick and Bucket said about having more electric appliances, like a fridge. His system was simple, so far, just direct current to the greenhouse fan. That made sense since he'd need the fan through the heat of the day. He would have to upgrade to a battery power system for the rest of the year when sunlight was weaker and available for shorter periods. Then he could have lights, a stereo, even a washing machine or blender if he wanted. That would run into some money. What he had now was a hand-me-down system from Chick upgrading his own system. The newer panels were more efficient and tougher. A fridge, anyway, would be nice. Henry wanted to be a little more diverse in his cooking, but was limited by food storage options. He remembered something else from the evening before and went inside.

His backpack was where he left it on the table. He opened it and fished out the loot he won in the Barter Round of the poker game. From Dave he got a set of old handcuffs, with key, Cash drew a picture of a dart board with darts to be delivered when convenient, Chick had bet a handmade halibut lure, and Bucket scrawled "wine cooler" on a piece of paper. Henry had thought he meant the bottled wine cooler drinks since Bucket brews his own beer and dabbles in wine, mostly for Sleet, but in the singular may mean an appliance for keeping wine cool. As in a small refrigerator. Which reopened the debate. Even if he didn't upgrade the system, he really didn't need refrigeration so much in the cooler months. In fact, he remembered an article in one of the *Whole Earth* catalogs about insulated cellar pits that would solve the problem year-round.

He began to form the idea in his mind to figure out what he wanted to fix up the house and to just do it already, for Pete's sake, but realized he would have to save up for it. He didn't have money to throw around anymore. Which brought him to G. Buckmeister Hill. He had said he would think about it, and here he was thinking about it. When he picked up his backpack to hang it up, the open compartment opened further and the card he bought fell out and glided under the edge of the kitchen cupboard. A. J. He was thinking about her a lot, too. He bent down and reached for the card. As it slid out from under the edge of the cupboard, a small capsule rolled into view. It was a Zoloft. The one he set out to take with breakfast, but forgot about. In March. He hadn't felt the need for one since.

*Snow was falling thick and swirly from a black sky and Henry couldn't find his car. There were huge domes of snow in the parking lot and any one of them could be it. He began shoveling away the base of the first dome. It didn't look familiar, but he kept working. He cleared enough snow away to open the driver's door and Ms. Walton sat serenely behind the wheel, thanking him for being so kind. He went to the next car. This one looked vaguely familiar and had a license plate he recognized. When he got the door open, his father had just started the engine and was chewing him out for not doing all the neighbors' walks first since that was a paying job. The next car was harder to dig out because it felt like the snow was falling faster than he could remove it. When he finally got the windows clear and could see inside, he saw A. J. as a young teen curled up on the back seat. He pried open the door, slid in and pulled her close to warm her, but she wouldn't wake up.*

Buttercup met Henry on the porch when he got back from dumping the morning's coffee grounds on his compost pile. She sniffed where he'd sat on the step in his slippers and fleece to write what turned out to be a four-page letter to A. J. It was folded and stuffed in the envelope with the Dyea watercolor card and stamped, ready to mail.

"Good morning, Buttercup. It's still a little early for the turkey rodeo. Want to go for a walk?" She did. They walked quietly past the tepee, gauging their pace to the rhythmic snoring inside, went out the drive and turned left. In one of the wider dandelion patches beside the narrow road, the black sow and her cub were biting off the flower tops and barely looked up as Henry and Buttercup padded past. On the main road, they strolled toward the Taiya River bridge. The sound of a car made them stop and turn. It was Chick on his way to work in town. He stopped and rolled down his window. Buttercup wagged her tail.

"Hey, you two. Nice morning."

"Hey, Chick. Early bird gets the worm. Would you mail this for me?" Henry handed Chick the A. J. letter. "I'm afraid if I wait till I get to town I'll lose my nerve and tear it up."

"Ooh, I'll drop it off before work, make sure nothing happens to it. Everything okay?"

"Yeah."

"Pick you up early Thursday if the weather's good?"

"You bet. I have a new halibut lure to try out." Chick smiled, waved and drove away.

"We'd better get to work, too, Buttercup. Turkeys to wrangle, biscuits to eat, garden to tend. Busy, busy, busy." When they got home, they could hear Squint in the house, singing. Something from Carmen, Henry guessed. Since Ms. Walton gave him his own razor, he, like Henry, kept a clean-shaven face. After a night in the tepee, he heated water first thing in the morning for shaving. They often shared the water. Henry opened the pen and the coop, then stood back. The turkeys always looked surprised by the world outside the coop and took a few minutes to remember what to do in all the space. Buttercup's one woof seemed to ground them and they settled down to scratching for and finding and eating worms and bugs.

"Did you already have coffee, brother?" On the porch, Squint wiped his face and draped his towel over his shoulder. "I didn't dump the wash water yet if you want it."

"Thanks. Yeah, I was up early." Henry went inside, lifted the wash pan out of the sink and rinsed out the coffee pot to fill. "I'll make another pot. I wrote a letter to my daughter and caught Chick to mail it for me." Henry opened double Ziplocs and took out a handful of biscuits for Buttercup. "It really helped me to think through an offer I got." He told Squint about meeting Mr. Hill and getting an offer for a job.

"But you have a job," Squint said. They sat on the step. "And isn't it better to work with people whose eyes you can see?"

Henry knew what he meant. Understanding and doing anything productive across time and space was a different relationship than face to face. It was isolating and involved assumption and conjecture. And like Squint's former partnership with Sister Mary Reginald, faith and trust. "That is a very good point."

"Lily says her paint should be here this week. We can start her house." Henry had forgotten about Ms. Walton's paint job. When she picked up her new glasses and went home, she was horrified by the view from her driveway. She called the hardware store and ordered paint for the house the next morning. She picked periwinkle, according to Squint, with sunflower for the trim. She liked the blue she had, but wanted more color. Squint had been chipping away at the peely parts and getting it ready to paint. Henry offered to help and followed the scraping with sandpaper. He was working on the porch when Ms. Walton got into her garden with a rake. She cleaned out a huge, overgrown raspberry patch and rhubarb area, then scratched all around the stone head. Henry took the opportunity to ask who the stone figure was. She said she didn't know anything about it, it was there when she bought the house. But she liked that the top of the head was flat enough to hold a flower pot. She looked at the figure and tipped her head. She set down her rake and ran into the house. She came out with the snorkel mask she wore the first time Henry met her. She knelt and stretched and cajoled the mask onto the head. She recovered her rake and went back to work.

Squint's Tuesday art student and Widge arrived together around nine. Henry had dressed and was busy in the greenhouse. The artists carried sketch pads to go work in the sun on the tideflats and Widge started work in the coop. He came flying out a minute later.

"An egg! Henry, we got an egg!" Widge had straw on his clothes and in his hair and held the egg in both hands out in front as he crossed the pen and met Henry.

"Hey, this one is bigger than the last one you found. Is it a Narragansett or Red?"

"Oh, shit! I'm supposed to keep track of that for my 4-H report. I think it was the scraggly Narragansett. They don't stay in their own boxes, so I don't know how I'm supposed to really know. But isn't it a beauty? Let's eat it."

"I don't know, Widge, it's pretty valuable just to eat."

"You're right. I should trade someone for something."

"Or you could give it to someone."

"Oh. I could give it to you, but it's already half yours because we're partners. Who would you give your half to?"

Henry squatted next to Widge and touched the egg. "I'd give my half to Ms. Walton."

"Ms. Walton!? Why?"

"Well, she likes fresh eggs and because she lives next door to a turkey ranch and has to put up with the occasional, you know, ranch sounds. You may not have noticed, but she's a lot easier to get along with now that she can see and she's taking Squint's herbs."

"She could probably use a bucket of manure, too."

"I'm sure she could."

"Mom wouldn't mind me going there if I took a gift. Would you go with me?"

"I'd be honored."

Ms. Walton loved the gifts and loaded Widge down with chocolate-dipped raspberry shortbread cookies. On the walk back, he'd counted the cookies and decided how many he could reasonably eat and still take a credible number home without his mother suspecting how many he ate. Then he asked Henry if he could help paint the house. He put his loot in the cabin and went back to cleaning "la maison de la dinde," as his father had called it when they built it. The name came from a discussion of what "pardon my French" means.

In the afternoon, Henry had just stretched out on his couch for a nap, when an engine sound was followed by heavy steps across his porch and in the open door.

"Hank, I could use a hand with something. Are you sleeping on such a beautiful day?" Darwin made a beeline for the sink. "Man, I need a drink of water. What's this, a new dog biscuit? Mmm, it's good. I like this one better than those sissy pumpkin ones."

Henry got up and stretched. "Darwin, what's up?" He studied the back and top of Darwin's head, rolled back as the boy guzzled water from a glass. "Is that a real haircut?"

"Whoo, I needed that." He turned and leaned his hip into the counter. "Yeah, pretty fancy, huh? Calliope cuts hair. You should go see her. Only four days to the big solstice bash on the flats, I'm gathering wood for the bonfire. Driftwood's a nice idea, but for quality of the fire and ease in feeding it, it's better to bring clean wood and have it in a neat stack ready to go." He regarded Henry. "What, are you a beach bonfire purist?"

Henry smiled. "I'm sure you've forgotten a lot more about beach bonfires than I'll ever know."

"Well, I figured you had nothing better to do today. Remember where we cut up West Creek Road? There's a big pile of odds and ends that will look sort of like driftwood, not too tidy, like we're using Presto Logs or something, and clean up that site. Win, win. You in?"

"Yep. See, there you go. I didn't know party bonfires had such important aesthetic issues." He put on his boots and looked for work gloves.

"Pfft. I guess it's been awhile since you've been involved in a beach party. We used to use pallets, but there was the sea of nails problem. After a few dozen flat tires, a guy gets over that. Besides, people are using them for other things now, useful stuff."

The road up the hill was still soft from spring break-up, but firm enough to drive up to the site, turn around and load the truck. They wrestled the uneven chunks quietly for the most part, but now and then Darwin whistled a piece of a Disney-sounding tune. On the way down the hill, he did it again. Henry looked at him and grinned. Darwin noticed. "What?"

"Nothing." Henry looked out his window to hide the smile on his face. "It's just that you look so happy. I'm really glad to see it. Did you get a puppy or something?"

"Nah, I don't know.... things are going pretty well lately. Don't laugh, but I just filled out all the paperwork yesterday to apply for the maintenance job open at the municipality."

"Holy shit, Darwin. Regular hours, someone else's agenda, no spitting? What brought that on?"

"Well, it was a bunch of things. You know I like to do my own stuff, but I wouldn't mind taking it a little easier. Have days off. Holidays, even. Get some damn insurance. I keep thinking, what happens if I break my leg or something. I'd starve. I actually had a dream about that, it was pretty scary. Then I was also thinking about my dad's house in town. It's good for me, alone, but.... So I decided to rent it out for the summer. There's good money in that."

"And you can spend more time out here with Calliope."

"Yeah. Have you really looked at that place? The house is in great shape and there's room for a couple cabins behind it. She wants me to build them. And with the trees, there's really only good light in a small area, so we did a vertical garden thing using pallets. Chick set up a heat pump watering system. You should go see it." Darwin glanced at Henry. "Are you giving me a hard time about her? Mr. Stay-over-Sunday-nights-with-Minerva?"

"No, I'm happy for you. She's really something. And she makes you look better, and I don't just mean your hair. What do you hear about Minerva and me?"

"Nothing. Well, first everyone was surprised because they still thought she was a lesbian. When she came to town she came with a friend and since they lived and worked together and didn't respond to the generous local male hospitality, we all assumed they were a couple. The friend left within the year and she never dated anyone. Until you. Now we all just wonder, since she hasn't had anyone in so long, if she's wearing you out." Darwin paused. "How're you holding up?"

Henry laughed. "I don't want to take all the wonder out of aging, you wait and find out for yourself." They'd just broken out of the trees into brilliant sunshine on the narrow road out onto the tideflats and could see someone waving arms above a mostly bald head. "Speaking of older gentlemen keeping company with cultured women, there's Squint."

"Yeah, that's another whack upside the head isn't it, him and Ms. Walton . . . What the hell is he doing?" Darwin stopped and they both got out.

"Over here! Come look!" Squint hopped up and down in excitement and waved the two men over a series of old, overgrown sandbars. Henry inhaled salty air and tried not to step on small pink and purple pea-like flowers in a tangle of greenery. They reached a spot where Squint's student was sitting with her sketchpad on her knees, drawing the tableau in front of her. Darwin and Henry both gasped when they recognized the centerpiece. It was the shaft and worn fletches of a green arrow. The tip was buried in a piece of wood.

"I'll be damned, Squint, you old bloodhound! Will you look at that? You gonna tell Widge?" Darwin gently touched the top of the arrow. It barely moved, the point securely embedded. "I hope this isn't historic wood."

"What do you mean?" Henry asked.

"The kid's been in enough trouble with his family, he doesn't need to get busted for shooting an artifact. Park Service. Never mind." They all stood looking at the arrow. Henry offered an idea.

"How about we leave it, then when everyone's here at the solstice party, we steer Widge over here to find it." Henry could imagine how the boy would react to finally getting the key to get out of the doghouse.

"I like it," Darwin said. Squint nodded approval. "But let's tell Chick and Lorelai. They'll get a kick out of setting him up."

The art student set down a pastel crayon and began smoothing colors together. The three men leaned in to see her drawing. It was riot of greenery around the sides, coiled like razor wire with little thorn-like points. Scattered in the green were bright purple and pink flowers with tiny faces, all puckered in anxiety. The chunk of wood had a rich grain in shades of gray and was shaped like a heart. The arrow nearly vibrated in its sharp clarity and there was a dribble of bright red where it pierced the wood. The young woman hunched over her work seemed oblivious to the three art critics taking a respectful step back. Squint made eye contact with the others and simply shrugged.

# 15

Clouds piled in quickly and quietly Wednesday evening threatening rain. The forecast was for about a thirty percent chance of showers, which Henry came to believe was a standard guess not too far from zero in case nothing happened. Which had been the case for a few weeks. The forest was getting dry and Squint shared a worry that the berry crop may suffer. It really looked like rain when Henry went to bed, but he planned to get up early and be ready to go fishing on Thursday anyway. Around four in the morning when he walked to the outhouse, the ground was wet. The forest smelled fresh and green beneath a very pale sky. The sun had just begun lighting up the valley and didn't have a lot of power behind it yet, but there was not a cloud within sight and not even a hint of a breeze.

Henry finished a stovetop quesadilla when Chick drove up. "How long will we be out?" He was thinking about food as he stuffed a jacket in his pack with a hat and gloves.

"Long enough to get a couple of fish. Lorelai packed us a thermos of coffee and some sandwiches. Everything else is on the boat. Oh, bring a water bottle, I guess. I got some herring out of the freezer." Henry put on his rubber boots, grabbed sunglasses, made sure he had his fishing license and was ready to go. The drive into town was breathtaking. The air was clean from the rain and Henry could see every tiny shrub, rock and snow patch detail of the Dewey Peaks above Skagway. The only sign of life in town was other people getting their boats ready to take out of the harbor.

By mid morning, hot sun had the fishermen's boots off and feet up on the rail of the drifting Bayliner. Their rods, stuck into holders on the stern, were rigged for halibut with lines sunk into an alleged halibut hole. Chick showed Henry a book with chart pages marked with such holes. Lynn Canal, a fjord, was incredibly deep and would seem to be a hotbed of anything that liked the bottom of really deep places. He asked, "Does this really show where the halibut are?"

Chick shook his head. "Maybe, I guess. I don't know. Some people only fish over places as deep as they're willing to pull something up from, don't really care where it is, and catch fish. Others study the charts, plot and plan and never catch a thing. I don't put as much strategy into it as a lot of people do. Fish will take my lure or not and hang onto it long enough for me to wrestle them in, or not. Otherwise, I enjoy being out here." He pointed down the fjord. "There's another whale spout."

Humpback whales were a thrill for Henry. He and Chick had looked for them in May while salmon fishing, but hadn't seen any. Glassy flat water made them visible from far away. They could hear the whoosh as well as see the plume of vapor from the huge marine mammals surfacing to breathe. Now and then they saw the flukes of a massive tail. Henry was struck by the contrast to the day he arrived in February. Same place, same water, but what a difference. It had been gray, cold, clammy, and windy. Today was anything but. He wiggled his toes and shifted in his chair. His tee shirt hung over the back of the chair and his pants were rolled up to his knees – not at all what he pictured fishing in Alaska would be like. "It's too bad Widge couldn't come today, this is perfect."

"Yeah. But it's worth a couple more days being grounded for him to find the arrow at the party. It'll save him having to hunt everyone down to tell them about it. He really has been looking for the damn thing. You don't know how many times I wanted to give him a break."

"I bet. He's a great kid. Smart, funny...kind hearted. Willing to help anyone anywhere. Swears a blue streak, though. Do all kids talk like that now?"

"Well, they do, but not as much as he does at nine years old." Chick shook his head. "It's my fault, but we think he'll grow out of it. So we're trying not to draw too much attention to it."

"How is it your fault, you hardly swear at all."

"Oh, I made a conscious effort to clean up my mouth. It was about three years ago now, I had a bad year. Lorelai and I were both were real busy, took on too many things, and I thought.... Well, I thought she was seeing someone else. I didn't realize I was swearing all the time until my sweet little boy started spewing the same language. Lorelai ripped me a new one and I lashed back at her, but she managed to make me understand what was going on with her, with us and with our family. Now Widge really only does it when he gets excited, but as you know, he gets excited a lot. It's kind of a family joke. Ruby's been working with him, bless her heart. Anyway, since I brought it up, my wife was not seeing someone else. She just isn't always in love with me. Her words." Chick gave Henry a serious look. "That ever happen to you?"

Henry thought a long moment. "In all honesty, I don't believe my wife was ever in love with me. She had this plan for her life and I was part of it. Until I wasn't. I had a girlfriend after that. She was nicer to me, generally, but I don't think she loved me, either. No, I'd have to go back to college and Ellen Dieffenbacher." He sighed.

"She sure made me think she loved me, and I still dream about her, but you gotta wonder why I never saw her again after finals."

Chick shook his head slowly for a moment then busted out laughing. "Holy moly, that is the worst story I've ever heard!" They both laughed. "You making any progress with Minerva?"

"More than I deserve, probably. No, certainly more than I deserve." Chick was clearly expecting more. "As you know, she speaks her mind, so when she says she wants me there for supper, I believe she wants me there. I find that refreshing and...uplifting." They both snickered. "And when she asks me to stay over, I believe she wants me. For a guy my age and in my circumstances, that's pretty damn good."

"But do you like her?"

"Yes, I like her. She's positive, can speak well on any subject, and she says what she means. I don't have to try to guess. She loves her life and the people around her and she's...beautiful. She's really a striking woman. With a killer voice. I truly enjoy every minute of her company, however she chooses to share it. I flipped my mattress for her."

"So, you ARE getting laid." He sighed. "Darwin and I had a bet."

"You know what, though? I can't stop wondering why she picked me. Am I safe? Unthreatening? Easy to manage? I asked and she said I'm a good neighbor and a good listener. And generally smell good. Is that all women want?"

"Nah, she's just messing with you. What do you care? You like her, she likes you, you have a good time. Did you think you'd meet anyone here?"

"No. Not in a million years. I keep wondering if I'm imagining her. Or my relationship with her. Maybe she's at the police station right now getting a restraining order."

"Well, you can never totally rule that out. Hey, there's another whale!"

By midday they had two halibut. Chick judged them to be about forty pounds each, the perfect size, he said. The slightly larger one was caught on Henry's new lure. They put away the gear and turned for home as a breeze freshened from the south.

"If you don't mind me asking, Chick, what's your retirement plan?"

"You mean, do I have one? More or less. I plan to retire from the power company in five years. I figure I can do some consulting around the state after that, help Lorelai at home so she can spend more time on her pottery. I'd like to set up a solar and wind home kit business, but will have to see how the money goes. Ruby's off to college this fall and we've got the Widget for about ten more years."

"Then you've got him to put through college."

"That's pretty well taken care of. Lorelai's uncle left a trust fund. He was kind of a rich bastard in Fairbanks, where she grew up. He taught me to fly and was real supportive when we got married, but was disappointed that we had a daughter first. Like we could or would select for a boy. Anyway, he set up a fund for our first boy's education. He died before Widge was born and we sure could have used the money for other things, but the fund was airtight, so it's there for him. Anyway, I've got a 401(k) that I may need to convert to something else. Maybe you can help me with that. What have you got?"

"Social security."

"That's it?"

"Yep. And lucky to have it. Don't ever think you can outsmart the Securities and Exchange Commission. With Regulation D, anyway. At least not forever."

"Got it."

"Just the other day, though, I ran into a guy in the bookstore I used to know. He wants me to consult for a group of investors he's in."

"Would it be worth your while?"

"There's a lot of money in money."

"But..."

"Right. That's what I keep thinking about." They slowed to enter the now buzzing harbor. "I'd be happy to look at your retirement account, see what you've got."

"Okay, thanks. I'd be happy to set you up wireless off Ms. Walton's system. You've got plenty of juice to run a laptop. Get you on Facebook, anyway, so you can communicate around here. Get the news. Stuff like that. You pay half her bill, you'd be doing her a big favor. She pays too much for what little she uses it for. Just downloads music, as far as I can tell. You can probably have Ruby's old laptop."

Dodging buses and pedestrians, Chick stopped in town only long enough for Henry to run upstairs to the newspaper office and invite Minerva out to the Devines for grilled halibut. At the north end of State Street, out of the flurry of cruise ship traffic, they also stopped at the health food store for rice flour and oats for the dog biscuit factory. Chick assured him Lorelai had everything else for dinner. Even wine. She traded Bucket a set of plates she made for about a gallon of what she said was a very decent dry white.

The fish was grilled with herbs from the Devine greenhouse and Henry got the cheeks. The sweet, tender meat reminded him of scallops. He ate one and insisted Minerva have the other. They cooked the smaller of the two fish and Henry got a lesson in butchering halibut earlier in the day helping Chick cut and wrap the second one for the freezer. They really only cooked half the smaller fish, the rest was put into a brine for smoking. That was something else Henry had wanted to learn. He toured the greenhouse with Lorelai after Minerva arrived. She showed them how her hydroponic system worked. Henry asked if she'd help him set up a similar system for his vegetables next year. That would free all his soil for flowers.

## Nowhere Else to Go, but Dyea

Over dinner at the outdoor table, Minerva shared the sad news that His Honor had died in his sleep the night before. She spent the morning looking for relatives and writing his obituary. No known family, but everyone she talked to in town had a story about him. He had a will and left everything to the day care center, according to Ruthless Red, though it would have to be verified legally. He didn't want a service, but everyone agreed a modest memorial at the solstice party was something he wouldn't mind. Minerva waited for Widge to run to the house for the cranberry cream pie to add, "There is a rumor going around that His Honor will be attending the party. Dave promised to keep a close eye on Bucket."

"What's a memorial?" Widge asked when he got back with the pie and a can of whipped cream.

"Like a funeral, but more casual," Ruby explained. "Without the casket and burial. This soon after he died, we could call it a wake. But that's usually just a drinking party. Anyway, at a memorial people tell stories, or sing or play music. They usually toast the person."

Widge's face reflected wonder, horror and fascination. "Toast, like toast?"

Chick stood up and raised his wine glass. "No, they say nice things, like this. Here's to your mother, the most beautiful woman in the world, a fabulous potter, gardener, and accomplished pie maker." Henry, Minerva and Ruby stood, raised their glasses and responded, "Here, here!"

Widge watched and listened, wide-eyed. "But what if the person isn't any of those things? What if you didn't even like them?"

Lorelai said, "Remember when the mean chicken with one wing that none of us liked died and we had the funeral?" Widge nodded. "We stood around the grave and said things like, 'she was a good clucker,' and 'she could sure turn left.' Well, it's the same for a person's memorial. Everyone thinks of something they were good at or said that was funny, and we all share it so we can remember them fondly."

Buttercup had spent the dinner period under the table, but walked out from under it into a long stretch, yawned and leaned against Widge's knee. He thoughtfully rubbed her ears. "So when Buttercup dies, we'll have a memorial for her and everyone will say things like what a good turkey guard she was or how she saved Albedo." The adults and Ruby got into it and each contributed a special quality or act of bravery to add to Buttercup's future memorial.

Minerva had planned to go back to town after dinner and keep working on the next issue of the paper, but relaxed and had another glass of wine, then with just a little more coaxing, agreed to stay with Henry and get an early start in the morning. The two of them walked out to the flats after washing the dinner dishes and stopped to watch the black sow nurse her cub in a patch of Angelica. After nursing, the sow curled around her baby and fell asleep. The humans tiptoed past and continued out toward the beach. Minerva asked if he'd ever seen anything so wild and beautiful.

"Easy one," Henry said. "The northern lights the first time you came to my house. You said the trees were too close to see it all, so we skied out to just about here and flopped down in the snow to watch the show."

"Okay, you're right, that was about as wild and beautiful as it gets. I'd never seen them run like that before and I'd never seen red."

"I'd have to call a nursing and napping bear family a close second to that."

Henry found and showed Minerva the green arrow and told her the plan for Widge at the solstice party. She loved it. They went as far as the water's edge and Minerva's skirt pocket bleeped. She took out her phone and pushed buttons. "It's from my intern." She began a series of return texts with bleeps in between. "Oh, you know Catalina? She just signed herself 'Catatonic,' the little smart-ass, having to start the layout without me. She can really do all this, just likes to make me feel needed, I think. I still write all the headlines because they're fun, but she's writing just about all the text this summer. And taking most of the photos. Okay, done." She dropped the phone back in her pocket.

On the way back to the cabin, Henry told Minerva about fishing with Chick. That the water was flat and it was quiet and beautiful and that they saw whales.

"What did you talk about all day?" She untied a pink silk shawl from her waist and wrapped it around her bare shoulders.

"Oh, nothing, really. Family, retirement. You know. He says he can run WiFi off Ms. Walton's service for me." At her glare under a raised eyebrow, he cracked. "Okay, we did talk about you." She smiled. "I shared that I don't deserve the attention you give me and that I'm grateful for every bit of it." She slid her arm around his middle and kept walking.

"There was one other thing we discussed that you might find interesting," he said. "That sometimes one person who is committed to another doesn't love that person all the time. I never thought about it that way before. I remember reading an article about Mother Teresa. She said she lost her faith for years, but kept up her work because it was the right thing to do. Later, she said, her faith came back. What a lesson in patience, for one thing, but in knowing what you want and need in this life, what you're willing to give. We marry and set up joint lives based on a basic promise to love forever. No wonder half of our marriages end. But more than that, we think we're unhappy when the person who is basically our business partner stops, or says she has stopped, loving us." He was thinking about Anne and Claire, neither of whom he actually missed personally.

"I believe you're right," Minerva said and took a deep breath. "You've surely heard by now that I came to Skagway with a partner. We were good friends in college and kept in touch over the years, cheered and consoled each other through romances and projects, then we worked together at a time when we were both feeling alone and broken-hearted. I thought men had nothing to offer me and was happy to give them up. So was she. We were in our forties and there were doubtless some hormone issues involved. After a couple years, this opportunity opened and I wanted to take it. She had nothing better going on, so invested and came with me. It was my dream job, not hers, and she wasn't happy here. And therefore, no longer happy with me. I was really hurt at first, but realized I truly had my dream job and was starting to build a nice life. I no longer needed or wanted her. So she left, I bought her out, and we're still friends. The upshot is, I learned a thing or two about the holistic nature of happiness. We've heard since the Sixties that you have to love yourself before you can love another. It's complicated and yet it's not. Even loving a puppy can be confusing. Are you really loving the puppy or some character trait present or missing in yourself? Then humans get so tangled up in sex they often miss the whole point of a social experience."

"Well, as one who is fumbling for the reset button on his entire social exper–. Listen...do you hear that?" They were stopped at the end of the shared part of Henry's and Ms. Walton's driveway and could hear a Strauss waltz coming from the piano. It was so rich and complex, it had to be four-handed. "Do you waltz?"

"Not recently." She took the hand he offered and gamely followed over the rough surface of the road. He gently twirled her up his drive and into his yard, once around the tepee and to the porch. She giggled the whole way.

He kept her hand and led her up the steps. "You are a delightful, multi-sensory experience, Minerva."

"You make my whole brain light up, too, Henry."

# 16

Minerva was a practiced and thorough sleeper. Henry watched her with some envy. Her face, propped on his shoulder, glowed with serene, deep peace. He had a full bladder and needed to move. He slowly slid out from under her head while replacing the space he vacated with a pillow. She took one slow, deeper breath and adjusted to the new situation, sliding her knees up into a fetal position. Still asleep. Still beautiful.

After a quick dash to the outhouse, Henry started coffee. He went to the greenhouse and carried the now blooming potted peonies to the porch. He snipped off a handful of flowers and brought them inside, scattering them over his sleeping beauty. The coffee perked, he turned it very low. It was still early and he felt no compulsion to wake her. He slipped on pants and a tee shirt and jogged in his slippers over to the Divines. Minerva's Subaru key was in the ignition as he'd hoped. Lorelai came out of her greenhouse and waved when he turned the car around so he stopped to speak with her.

"Are we on for smoking the halibut today? I'd really like to take it to the solstice party." Henry realized he was whispering.

Lorelai whispered back, "Come over as soon as she leaves, we'll fire up the smoker."

Henry parked the Subaru by the woodshed and tiptoed into the house. She had turned over, but was still asleep. He put a pan of water on the stove to heat up for bathing. He set out a clean towel and lined his toothbrush, paste and comb next to it in case she wanted to use them. A thump on the porch told him Buttercup was ready to work. He took a cup of coffee and a few dog biscuits outside, released the turkeys and sat on the porch. Friday, June 20th was going to be another lovely day.

After Minerva gulped down coffee, washed her face and ran a comb through her hair, she kissed Henry, patted Buttercup and was gone. He cranked up the radio to listen to news while he made the bed and tidied up. The weather could go either way over the next few days and many issues were hot in Skagway and Haines politics. As in an average day. There was a short news item concerning the death of Mr. Calvin Hochstatler, longtime resident and former magistrate of Skagway. A tipster had called in that Mr. Hochstatler's entire property in midtown Skagway was wrapped in police tape, details were expected for the noon news broadcast.

Henry assumed the deceased was His Honor and wondered what was up with his property. He remembered seeing the house a time or two as he walked or biked between the library and grocery store. The fence surrounding the half block was taller than everyone else's fence. Even on tiptoe, Henry couldn't see over it, so it must be a little over six feet high. And solid. Vertical wood slats overlapped and didn't allow any spying. The garage door and one gate were the only way in to the Victorian style house with a cupola above the second floor. From the cupola a person could see the entire neighborhood, but no one on street level could see onto the property. It seemed kind of odd to Henry since most homes were much more welcoming with low fences, walkways and welcome mats.

After Widge arrived to do his chores, Henry hustled back to the Devines to begin learning to smoke fish. Chick and Ruby were gone to work and Lorelai had the brined fish and racks out on the back porch next to the smoker. She gave Henry a quick tutorial on where to plug in the smoker so the breeze won't fill the house with smoky fish smell, how to wet what kind of chips, how to rack the strips of fish and how to load the smoker. About half their fish fit on the racks for the first batch.

"That's it," she said. "Let's check on it in about six hours. I'll put the rest back in the fridge, we can do a second batch later or tomorrow if you want."

"That's all there is to it?" Henry was a little disappointed.

"Well, everyone has their own recipe for the brine, but unless you're going old style with homemade outdoor racks and an open fire, it's pretty easy. If you weren't ever going to use your tepee for anything else, it would make a good smoker."

"Huh. Okay, I'll be back in six hours. Thank you for this." Henry started down the road for home. About halfway to his turn-off, he heard a vehicle and turned to see Darwin slowing to a stop.

"Hank." The boy shut off the pick-up in the middle of the road and propped his elbow in the open driver's window. "You hear about His Honor?"

"Yeah, I did. I'm sorry, I know he was your friend."

"Well, he was pretty damn old."

"What do you think the story about police tape around the whole property is all about?"

"I'm skipping yoga class right now to go find out about that. When I was a kid he was always real good about finding jobs for me to do and paying me. He's got this huge yard and he had it staked and marked out with string in a grid, said he was planting an orchard and needed a lot of holes dug. Later, since he was having me dig holes between the trees, he said he was doing secret archaeological work. I must have dug about a hundred holes for him. Thought I'd better go see Dave."

"Jesus, Darwin."

"Can you go with me? We'll stop by your house. Get your boots." Henry looked down and noticed he was still in his slippers. At his house they grabbed gloves and shovels.

By noon, Dave, Darwin, Henry, and Ruthless Red's two teenage sons had dug eight tidy rows of holes across His Honor's yard and dug around and under the roots of the cherry, pear and mountain ash trees. They had exhumed the remains of twenty-seven cats and eighteen rabbits. Dave was just getting into a local history lesson describing the tulip eating bunny and stray cat wars to Henry when one of the teens pulled a metal Jetsons lunchbox out of a hole in the ninth row, opened it and shrieked.

"You think you know someone," Darwin said as he made the turn around the head of Long Bay on the way home to Dyea. "He lied to me all those years."

"He was protecting you," Henry said. He picked up and unwrapped one of the burritos Dave got for them after declaring the digging over for the day. Dave and he were hungry enough to overlook the similarity between chili bean burritos and the burlap-wrapped bodies, but when he handed the warm bundle to Darwin, the younger man apparently wasn't and shook his head. Henry rewrapped it for holding and eating and took a bite. "He needed your help, you needed the job. Plus, according to Dave, people were mad enough to start using poisons on the strays. He was taking care of a problem that got out of hand and doing it humanely. Dave said they were all clean head shots."

"I remember several times my Dad said he was going to put out poison for the cats, but I don't think he ever did. They just disappeared. Now I know why. But all that other stuff...what was he doing?"

"One box was all cell phones, one was sunglasses. Two boxes of cameras. Dave guessed it was lost and found things from the visitor center. The box of pot and pipes that what's-his-name opened looked like confiscated stuff that never went to court. The gold rush artifacts may have been stolen or dug up, then no one knew where they came from to put back."

"Now Dave has to do something with it all. And we never would have known if the old man hadn't been in the middle of burying something, gone inside to lie down and died."

"Yeah, probably not. You've got to admire that lunchbox and fruit cake tin collection."

"See, that's what I remember, too, as a kid. He collected metal boxes. Now I know why."

"You can drop me at the Devines' drive, my halibut's probably shoe leather by now." Henry ate the last bite of his burrito and picked up the other one. "You want this for later?"

"No, you take it. I'm going to clean up and find something alive to hug."

Henry smiled. "Good plan. See you tomorrow. Come get me to help with whatever you do to get ready to celebrate the summer solstice."

"Will do, Hank."

Henry found Ruby at the smoker, sliding out the racks and poking the bits of fish. She saw Henry approaching and handed him a piece of hot fish. He nibbled cautiously, then gobbled the whole piece down.

"That is delicious! I thought it seemed like a waste to cut up and dry perfectly good fresh fish, but now I get it. I'd better try another one." He ate three more before Ruby got the racks emptied into a bag. She advised leaving the bag open to cool before closing it up. She offered to help Henry start the second batch of fish. She got it from the fridge while he washed up. As they worked, he asked her about school. She told him that she had been homeschooled since kindergarten, but that Widge went to public school. He asked why and she said homeschooling is a lot of work for the parents and not all kids are built for it. Widge liked going to school in town, but also spent time with Ruby's old books and workbooks, so he basically got a two-for-one. She said her mom and dad agreed it was best to keep him busy.

"We have a thing in the family about being busy or up to something. A lot of times, Widge will admit he's up to something when he should be busy."

"Speaking of whom..."

"He's in the shop, busy, actually. He's building a tiny coffin for His Honor. He and Mom came up with an idea for the memorial. You'll see tomorrow." She closed the smoker.

Henry picked up his burrito and first bag of fish to go home. "I thought I'd bring all this fish to the party tomorrow. Do you think that's enough?"

"Keep some for yourself. People will love it and eat it all if you don't. Someone always brings out a big grill and people cook chicken wings, brats, fish, stuff like that. We're taking lettuce wraps and some sausages Dad made last fall. Widge wants to kill and share his turkeys, but Dad talked him into waiting for Thanksgiving. Or at least Labor Day. He's saved a few eggs to take to Ms. Walton in the morning to make deviled eggs out of. I'm so glad he's not afraid of her anymore. We have you to thank for that. Anyway, we'll bring a box of plates, forks, towels, first aid. The band usually doesn't start until late, so we'll do the smores early enough so the little kids can go before then."

"When should I check on this batch?"

Ruby looked at her watch. "Let's put the timer on and it can shut itself off." She rooted in a drawer under the old table the smoker sat on and got a timer. They plugged it into the outlet and plugged the smoker into it. They agreed on a time and set it. "Just come and get it whenever you want and make sure everything is off."

Henry sat at his table to write in his journal but looked out the window instead. Rays of yellow sun came down through the trees around his yard. Green, turkey-trampled weeds covered the yard and colorful peonies hung from his porch roof. Squint suddenly popped out of the tepee carrying a sketch pad and walked down the driveway and out of sight. Henry wished he had wine or beer and someone to share it with, but settled for a cup of tea in the company of sunbeams.

*The snow was still swirling in the dark and Henry waited for the bus with Ellen Dieffenbacher. She had a pink silk shawl wrapped around her head and neck, but a few stray curls bobbed in the wind. He'd never noticed the gray in her hair before. She talked about visiting her family, getting started in her job, finding a place to live. He waited for an invitation to join her or a plan to meet somewhere later, but the bus arrived first and she was gone. In the dream, Henry took out a cell phone and called G. Buckmeister Hill.*

The man had just answered when he woke up. He put on sweats and slippers and went out to sit on the porch in the soft light of midsummer night. Henry had almost called Buck when they took a break from digging in His Honor's yard. Amid the piles of dirt, Henry had gotten a dizzying feeling of being at a dead end, having no future and dying alone with his closet full of skeletons. He borrowed Darwin's phone and took the business card out of his wallet. He started to dial. Dave got a call and had to run, so handed his clipboard to Henry. He stopped dialing and gave the phone back, said he'd try it later.

Slow, rhythmic snoring came from the tepee in the morning.

Squint had an early painting class on Saturdays and often slept there the night before. No sound at all came from the closed-up turkey house. Henry breathed the cool air, matching his own breathing to Squint's. The old man had a particularly slow respiration rate. Henry wondered if simple, clean living were responsible. Squint had his own skeletons and beat himself up over them for years, but he found positive things to do while working on forgiving himself. He told Henry once that thinking you killed someone is the same as really killing them. And that the real crime is letting yourself get to a place where you would do such a terrible thing. Deep down, we all know better, he'd summed up. Now Squint was sweeping that deep place with slow, cleansing breath. Henry closed his eyes and breathed with the former fugitive hermit, current singing, piano playing, house painting, fungus appreciating, Esperanto and Latin-speaking artist.

His butt was sore and cold when Henry opened his eyes. He'd heard something. It came again, a trill of a gobble from the turkey house. He'd heard it before and knew it meant there was a new egg. Widge would be pleased. Now that Henry's eyes were open, he noticed movement near the woodshed. The cinnamon bear cub stood up, then rolled over into the open. His black mother was right behind him, reaching out and gently cuffing her baby. Then she rolled, too, and they wrestled. Henry needed to stand up, but sat still and watched the bears roll and tumble. The turkey gobbled again and both bears stopped to listen for a moment, then got up and hurried into the forest.

When Squint came to the cabin for coffee and a shave, he whistled "Die Moldau". Henry had no idea why he recognized that tune, but whistled along and cooked breakfast. He had an idea earlier while slow breathing on the porch.

"You got any money, Squint?"

Without missing a stroke with the razor, Squint said softly,

"Money hasn't really been your best bedfellow, brother."

Henry laughed. "True, but just consider this. What if we pooled our money and built a real studio where the tepee is? You design it, make it however you want. Keep the dust and mold out of your stuff, racks for storage. A place to dry and store herbs. I'm saving more of my income than I expected to and I want to build something."

Squint stopped shaving, turned and beamed at Henry.

A raft of small rain clouds passed over Dyea midday and misted the valley for a few minutes. Workers barely took notice as they piled wood, set up benches and picked a spot for the band. The sound equipment would come later. Throughout the day, coolers filled with ice and beverages and food showed up and were left to themselves as people walked, rode horses, flew kites and enjoyed the longest day of the year. One cruise ship docked and kept shop and tour workers in town until later. A few vintage trailers and campers from Whitehorse set up near the party site with stretched awnings and extra chairs out for hospitality. Darwin was worried with so many people around that someone would find Widge's arrow. He and Henry discreetly piled seaweed and grass to hide it.

His Honor showed up in late afternoon, after most of the tourism business concluded for the day. A chair was set up for him on top of a big chunk of driftwood and his black robe draped over it, his hat set on the seat. Chick helped Widge place the little coffin in front of the chair with a pad of notepaper and a pen. A small sign invited people to leave a message for the former magistrate, mass cat and bunny murderer and town booster and place it in the coffin. It would be set on the bonfire later.

Henry went home around five to clean up and wait for Minerva. She got there before six and Henry was happy to see she brought an overnight bag. They walked out to the flats carrying his smoked halibut, a few bags of dog biscuits, her box of Shiraz, and a large Tupperware box of stuffed grape leaves.

Cars parked along the road and any available flat spot, people settled down to visit or headed off to play. Darwin started the fire earlier so there would be coals and a few people used sticks over the hot spots or fired up grills and began cooking. Everyone talked and laughed. Kevin and his family brought chairs and a bed for the baby. They also brought a bundle covered with a blanket. He set it near His Honor's chair and carefully unwrapped it. Everyone who was watching gasped. It was the Baby Jesus in his manger. Kevin arranged the blanket around it, turned and held up his hands.

"The deacons and I discussed this and decided that our little Christmas symbol has been telling us he shouldn't be locked away and protected, brought out only for Christmas. Just as Jesus broke out of his tomb, our little creche-meister has gotten around in spite of our efforts to keep him safe and taught is that he should be out more often and throughout the year." He looked down at a small child tugging on his pants leg. "Eulah Kathleen is going to be keeping an eye on Him, so wherever you are, Bucket, she's got your number." The crowd applauded.

Henry was offered a beer before he could share wine with Minerva, so decided to stick with beer. It was Bucket's current batch of spruce tip ale and Henry liked it. He also ate a turkey deviled egg Ms. Walton saved for him. He'd been disappointed his partnership with Widge in the turkey business hadn't earned him an egg yet, but after eating one, decided the highest and best use for the turkey eggs was to go to Ms. Walton. After Squint helped her get her egg trays and jug of highbush cranberry juice to the food area, he used pushpins from his pocket to tack a row of drawings on a driftwood log. His morning class drew their impressions of the summer solstice and wanted to share. Albedo tried to stay between Squint's feet and as soon as Ms. Walton sat, dashed under her chair. He was still uneasy outdoors. A fairly steady string of people took turns with the notebook and coffin and Henry noticed Ms. Walton cried while she wrote a lengthy note. She was wiping her eyes after she tore off and deposited her message and made eye contact with him. She came over to where he lounged with Minerva and sat beside them. Albedo slid in behind her legs and stuck his head out only far enough to lick Henry's offered hand.

"I am just sick about all the cats," she began. "If I'd known about the problem I would have gotten involved. But I was new here and had my own problems, I suppose." She heaved a big sigh. "What's done is done. Anyway, I couldn't have done without Calvin. He helped me with Mr. Walton's probate and then to clear up title to the house. He found the saintly woman who managed to do my blood-sucking taxes. And he introduced me to Yvo." Albedo slinked up into her lap.

It was Henry's turn at the little coffin. He took a slip of paper and began writing that he got it. He'd dismissed what the old man said when they met about many people having nowhere else to go as the general mood of a cold, gray, windy day, but now he saw it differently. As much as the physical location, where one lives is a three-dimensional map of the people; what they need from and give to each other. If you're lucky, having nowhere else to go means you're right where you belong. Henry thanked His Honor for introducing him to Darwin, his first friend, who introduced him to or gave him the courage to introduce himself to many other friends. He took the business card from his wallet, tore it in half and set it in the coffin with his note.

Henry got a signal from Darwin and nodded. Widge and Chick were walking back from the beach winding up a kite string. Henry walked casually to the arrow and uncovered it, then backed off. Darwin met Widge with the prearranged pretext of needing help gathering more wood. He pointed toward Henry who was bending and gathering sticks. Widge hopped and twirled, still flying his kite in his mind and worked his way toward Henry. Not watching where he stepped very well, he tripped and flopped down in the sand, into a patch of beach peas. He got up and leaned over to brush his pants off when he saw the arrow. His eyes wide as turkey eggs, he grabbed the shaft and pulled. The arrow came out and he turned to the party with it high over his head, a big smile on his face.

"Hey!" he yelled, "I found the fucking arrow!" As soon as the words were out, his jubilant look turned to one of horror and he clapped his free hand over his mouth. Lorelai, Chick and everyone else stopped breathing.

It was Bucket who stepped forward and held his beer glass high. "Here's to the fucking arrow!"

Ruby held up her cranberry juice and said the same thing. Sleet and Darwin were next, then individual salutes were lost in the crowd of raised glasses and cheers for the boy finding the arrow and redemption and hoping their solidarity would keep him from going right back in the doghouse with such a foul mouth. They would all work on that together. Chick scrambled over to the boy and hoisted him onto his shoulders. They did an impromptu arrow dance that many people joined in on. Henry sat and watched the wonderful way this community, his community, forgave each other their various crimes.

# 17

"I looked up your horoscope today," Minerva huffed, a cloud of vapor from her warm breath adding to the frost on the hair poking out of her scarf. "Do you want to know what it said?"

Henry glided two more steps on his skis to stop beside her in the late February afternoon gloom before answering. "I never paid much attention to it, having a real birthday only every four years. What'd it say?"

"It was long, so I'll paraphrase. You can't live up to or even really know the expectations of others, so you must identify and go after your expectations for yourself."

"That's it? Sounds like more of a fortune cookie – you made that up, didn't you?"

She laughed. "No, but I was disappointed, too. You deserve something more. Hey, maybe we should write a horoscope for the paper."

"Don't you have to know something about astrology?"

"Who says I don't?" The trail they followed through the forest was at times tortuous and crossed itself more than once. Widge made it as a memorial for Ruby while she was away at school. He was into memorials. The shorter loop between their houses was the

Buttercup and the one that crossed West Creek was the Flying Turkey. Minerva stopped. "Where the hell are we?"

Henry ducked down and looked between dark tree trunks. "See that shade of pinky blue? That's the back corner of Ms. Walton's. So we're almost home. I wanted to cook dinner for you, but Lorelai said they'd already planned a birthday dinner for me. I believe the last turkey will be involved. Maybe we can have a glass of wine before we head over to their house."

"I'm glad she invited us," Minerva said. "I'd rather be out skiing than inside watching you cook. Not that it isn't a pleasant thing. What were you going to make?"

"A baked egg thing kind of like quiche with last summer's dried mushrooms and herbs. Nothing special, really, but I'm learning."

"I look forward to having it another time." They ducked under low branches to stay on the trail. "Hold up a minute, I want to tell you something before we get back." She faced him and planted her poles. "I'm just going to say it. I've been corresponding with A. J. for a few months. I know you write to her and she doesn't write back. I think she just doesn't write that way. I tracked down her personal email and told her about you and how you live and how you've found a place in our hearts, and that we, many of us, are so happy you chose to live here." She watched his face.

He stared at her. "My A. J.?"

"Yes. And two things. She says you should incorporate The Dyea School of Atonement and Sustainable Living with Chick's Wind and Solar Kits for better tax advantage as soon as possible, even though you're still working out bugs, and she wants to hike the Chilkoot Trail with me this summer. She hopes you'll go along, too."

"She's coming here?" He felt a little dizzy. He wondered if he forgot to eat breakfast and lunch. He'd been busy helping Darwin and working on Chick's business plan and retirement adjustments.

He couldn't even imagine his daughter in this context. As a twelve-year-old she would have loved it, but now... She's right, he thought. Incorporating them together was a good idea. Non-profit and for profit parts of the same organization.

"She says it's on her calendar and I gather that's a big deal." She frowned up at Henry. "You should breathe for a minute, Stillwater. In... out... See, things always come together sooner or later, breathe in, breathe out..." They began moving again and he could hear Minerva giggling behind him. They broke out of the trees behind the woodshed and Henry saw cars in his yard. He expected Darwin's truck parked next to the new studio duplex he was building and Chick was teaching him to install solar panels on, and Minerva's Subaru, but there were several others. He heard a halloo behind him and turned to see Ms. Walton and Squint walking from her house.

"Hal, I was afraid we'd be late, but here you are!" She carried a tray and Squint had a bundle in his arms with a furry white muzzle sticking out the top. "We tried to leave Albedo home, but he insisted on coming."

On their knees on the porch, Bucket worked the crank on an ice cream maker while Sleet poured in rock salt. Henry and Minerva leaned their skis near the door which held a sign saying, "Happy Birthday!" and led the way into the bright, warm, wonderful-smelling cabin. Buttercup greeted Albedo under the table. Darwin ran the blender and poured cranberry margaritas. Chick slid a turkey out of the oven and set it on the table to rest. Lorelai adjusted rolls and pans of stuffing and mashed potatoes balanced on top of the wood stove. A woman stirred gravy in a skillet on the stove and Henry took a moment to remember her. She was the woman who lived on the other side of West Creek that he met when he was looking for Squint in the snowstorm. He realized he hadn't seen her since. How was that possible? Had he been that busy for the last year? Dave stood at the table frosting a cake. Cash set up a folding table and began unfolding chairs. Mrs. Cash sat in a corner of the sofa next to Calliope who massaged a bun in her oven; the eagerly anticipated Darwin, Jr. The old cabin was absolutely full of life. Everyone visited and went about their chores until Widge, who now rarely swore, but still couldn't stand suspense, weaseled through the crowd and handed Henry a package.

Perched on the arm of the sofa, Henry gently tore the wrapping from a cylinder-shaped thing. Free of the wrap it unrolled into a welcome mat with a yellow lab standing next to a turkey.

"Ruby and Esme found it at a yard sale near their school and thought of your porch," Lorelai said. "We had just talked on the phone and realized you never had a house-warming. Then somebody, Dave I guess, remembered your birthday is about now and we thought we should have a party for you. So happy birthday, Henry. And welcome."

# Acknowledgments

*Thanks to the following: Denny Bousson for his advice on Dyea living, Michael Yee for what goes into building a ski race aid station, Skip Elliott for explaining finances and the SEC, Jerry Gentile for poker and fishing tips, Danny Droege for raising heritage turkeys, and Kathleen O'Daniel for proofreading.*

A preview of Nita's next novel:

# The Dyea Convicted Felons Club

"Five card draw, gentlemen, ante up." Bucket began dealing five cards to each player. "This is like camping out under the stars, only better. Because you can see your cards."

"And you can smoke cigars while you cook," added Torch, twisting in his chair to reach back to the fire. He pulled out a burning stick and lit his cigar before tucking it back under the grill. "These dogs are getting crispy, anyone want another one?"

"Yeah, I'll take one," Darwin said, laying his cards face down as he got up.

Torch snorted around his cigar. "A sissy one with spinach in it?"

"Damn right," said Darwin. "First batch out of Calliope's vertical auto-water garden." He took a bun from the warmer crock next to the grill, opened it and used it like tongs to gently grab each dog and move it to the edge of the grill before selecting and taking one. The condiments were arranged on an upended piece of firewood next to the fire pit. He picked the Beaver cranberry mustard and squirted some on his bun before stuffing in the spinach. "How hard is it to grow mustard? We should make our own. A whole line of Dyea School of Atonement and Sustainable Living mustards. And horseradish."

"What do you say, Squint?" Henry discarded two cards and signaled to Bucket for two more.

"I'll look into it, brother. Three for me." Squint's formerly squinting eye bore into each player in turn as they looked at their cards. He was a summer-only participant in the weekly poker game and only played when it was held in Dyea. He tended to win more than anyone else, which would have made his invitation to play get lost in the mail, but he took it more seriously than the others. Early in the evening, at least. Until he got his pipe from his pocket and lit up. In the summer, old regular players like Dave, the cop, and Minerva, the newspaper editor, were too busy to play. Cash, the banker, really only liked to play when the game was in his garage in town. Rather, his wife really only liked him to play when the game was in his garage in town. Chick was traveling a lot, selling and setting up his solar kits, and his son Widge was grounded again and not allowed to stay up late enough to join the game.

"I fold." Darwin settled into enjoying his hot dog and suddenly felt the weight of a large furry chin on his knee. "Hey, Buttercup. You want a dog?" He got up and chose the charred hot dog furthest away from the heat, picked it up with his fingers to make sure it wasn't too hot and handed it to the big yellow dog. She wagged her tail a few lazy swings while she carefully took it in her teeth and headed to Henry's porch. She climbed the steps, lay down and thoughtfully ate the hot dog. That was her spot, on the porch. She only hung out under the poker table when she was trolling. As old and solid as she was, it was hard to beat her to pick up a dropped piece of anything good to eat.

"Does Buttercup ever go home anymore?" Torch lay his cigar on the edge of the table to pick up one new card.

## Preview - The Dyea Convicted Felons Club

"She's got a big job here lately with the chicken routine and training the new pup." Henry looked around. "Where is the new pup?"

"I got him," Squint said, nodding to the side and down without taking his eyes off his cards. Henry leaned to his left and looked under the table. A fuzzy yellow noodle drooped over Squint's bony knees. The pup's face sagged, a thread of saliva hanging from his lower lip. He was sound asleep.

"All worn out." Darwin shook his head. "Hey, it's not easy keeping up with all that goes on around here. Steep learning curve. He's training to be a chicken guard here, plus whatever else is on Buttercup's neighborhood route. Calliope says she saw a bear sniffing around her pallet garden yesterday and Buttercup came out of nowhere to run him off. The pup was right behind her. I guess I need to get a fence up around that damn garden." He sighed and sank further into his chair. "I gotta push off pretty soon, guys, I'm shot to pieces, too."

"Oh, you wuss." Torch had the winning hand and began scooping up chips. "You get a real job, get a woman, get a baby, pretty soon you don't have time for your friends and the manly game of poker." At Darwin's slow smile he added, "You lucky bastard."

Henry stood and stretched. "I'm getting stove up sitting. Maybe we should pack it in." The token grumbling around the table was just that. Everyone looked tired. Henry twisted his back side to side and looked around the yard, at the green hills above the trees leading to snowy mountains piercing the pale mid June sky. It was a beautiful evening after a warm, sunny day in Dyea, Alaska. The grass and dandelions around the edge of the yard were bright green and clipped low by the chickens and, obviously from the piles of poop, one or more bears. Buttercup, and now the pup, only ran bears off when they were too close to the greenhouse or gardens. The new structural addition to the compound, Henry admired with pride, was the studio duplex Darwin and he built out of lumber salvaged from a demolition project in Skagway. Chick was using it as a model to teach them to wire for solar and wind generation. Squint designed the building itself which included Pagoda style elements. As Henry looked at it, he considered where he could hang flower baskets. Squint's herb garden was starting to peek out of boxes on the studio porch between chairs he and his art students used on warm days. He was just about to ask Squint what tomorrow's class schedule was when he heard deep growling. He turned to his cabin and saw Buttercup on her feet, hackles raised and looking intently into the forest. She barked once and launched off the porch, charging into the trees behind the woodshed. The pup jerked awake and flopped to the ground, gathered his legs and fired off after her.

"The hell is that all about," asked Bucket. He had the chips in their box and the cards put away. "Sounded pretty serious. Like the night she took off and came back with that stringy little pup."

Darwin and Henry looked at each other. Bucket was right. They'd been playing cards in late May, the first outdoor game of the season. Everything seemed quiet, but Buttercup barked once and tore off into the woods. She came back leading a muddy, scared yellow lab puppy. The pup clearly had issues with people and took some coaxing to let the poker players look him over to make sure he wasn't injured, clean him up and give him something to eat. No one claimed him after diligent asking around and a note at the post office, but a claimant would have had a job of prying him away from Buttercup. She assumed responsibility and began the training program as soon as he was strong enough to keep up with her. He didn't have a name yet, but Henry, Squint and Darwin, his main uncles, knew the right handle would come when he was ready. Widge suggested Buttercup Junior, but was outvoted. For now, he was The Pup.

Everyone stood, listening for more information from the dogs. When it came, frantic barking from Buttercup and yipping from the pup, they all hurried into the forest, following the sound. After ducking under low branches and hacking through dense brush for just a few minutes, they came to an old, overgrown road and heard the dogs to the left. Looking through overhanging branches and leaning saplings, they saw a figure rise with effort from knees to feet and stagger toward them. Buttercup and the pup were on either side of it.

The figure had one arm clutched to his chest and batted at Buttercup with a small shovel held in the other. "Get away from me!" It was a man's voice and very agitated.

"Hey! Are you okay?" Darwin hollered. The figure stopped suddenly, legs planted far apart, reeled and fell over on his side. The poker players hurried to where the man fell and formed a ring around him, dropping to their knees. He had dirt smudges on his face and arms and whisps of hair jutted away from his center-bald head. Buttercup and the pup pressed in to lick his face when he moaned. Bucket and Torch, part of the volunteer fire department and both EMTs, began working on the man while the others pulled the dogs back.

"Hey, I know this guy," whispered Darwin. "He's a parky!"

"Hey, buddy! Can you tell us your name?" Bucket was in charge of the airway while Torch looked for injury and took a pulse. The man moaned again.

"Ah, shit," Torch said, "we need the ambulance. Darwin, can you get to a signal?"

"Yeah." Darwin got to his feet with the pup under his arm as Torch tried to pull the man's arm from across his chest

"No!" The man's eyes went wide, "They'll take it away!" He clasped the arm tighter and cried out in pain.

"Holy shit, what is this?" Torch saw the corner of a metal box wrapped in what looked like hide under the man's hand.

"It's mine! Mine!" Wild eyes focused on Bucket leaning over his face and the man repeated several times that he worked hard for thirty years and he deserved it. He yelled, "Don't let them take it away from me!" He stiffened and groaned, then went limp. Torch and Bucket began CPR. Darwin ran.

About twelve minutes later, Darwin jammed his truck into the ditch where the old road was barely visible from the main road to show the ambulance where to stop. He and the pup ran in to where CPR was still going on. "I got a call out, they're on the way. Is he . . .?" Torch and Bucket had handed off to Henry and Squint for a few minutes, then taken over again. Torch looked up at Darwin and shook his head, but kept working. The pup weaseled in close enough to sniff the man's leg, barked once, then moved back to sit next to Buttercup. The man's arms were flopped out to his sides and the bundle he'd held to his chest was lying beside him. Squint reached in and carefully drew it out. He, Henry and Darwin leaned down to look at it. Buttercup and the pup sniffed it. It was a metal box, about the size of a small lunchbox, with a wrapping partially stuck to it. Dirt and rust clumps fell away as Squint gently worked fingers around the lid.

"What do you think he meant about working thirty years and deserving this," Henry asked.

"He was supposed to retire this year," Darwin said. "Some mandatory thing. But something was screwed up with his retirement, I think. He was all pissed off lately, called in sick a lot." Everyone looked at him. "I hear things. City workers talk about the Park Service, parkies talk about city workers." Suddenly the metal box popped open and everyone gasped.

Bucket stopped chest compressions mid-stroke. "Holy shit, Dude, that was your retirement plan?"

Everyone stared wide-eyed except Squint. His formerly

# Preview - The Dyea Convicted Felons Club

squinted eye twitched and narrowed as he set the box on the ground and fumbled in his shirt pocket. He pulled out a pipe filled with the herb blend that made Lily Walton such a pleasure to live with, lit it, took a deep breath and passed it around. When he finally exhaled, he croaked, "'The stuff that dreams are made of' would be a gross understatement here, my brothers."

The Earth began spinning again with the sounds of the ambulance, emergency workers shouldering gear and hollering for directions. Darwin, Henry, Squint, Bucket, Torch, Buttercup and the pup leapt into action helping get the caregivers and all their gear to the patient and helping get it all back to the ambulance and away. Whatever the non-responsive parky had in his pockets and even the damn shovel made it onboard with their master, but the box . . . well, the box did not.

*Look for this future title from Lynn Canal Publishing.*

# Also by Nita Nettleton
*published previously by McRoy & Blackburn*

# The Wake Up Call of the Wild
# Accessories are Everything in the Wild
# Nature Runs Wild